PHANTOM DRIFT

A JOURNAL OF NEW FABULISM

ISSUE 7: *Creatures Born of a Long Denial*

Phantom Drift Limited
La Grande, Oregon

Issue Seven
Fall, 2017

PHANTOM DRIFT
A Journal of New Fabulism

ISSN: 2162-8211
ISBN: 978-0-9964426-2-6

Phantom Drift Limited is a 501(c)(3) tax-exempt organization founded to develop an understanding of and appreciation for fabulist literature. *Phantom Drift* is one of the few literary journals in the United States focused on fabulist writing. We aim to nurture the literature of fabulism, the fantastic, and the surreal by publishing an appealing, top-quality literary journal featuring only the best short stories, poetry, and critical thinking on fabulism by established, emerging, and new writers from the U.S. and abroad. Our support for writers takes the form of not only providing a showcase for their works, but offering payment, a practice that both assures us the best of writers' work and supports literature as a whole. The journal will be published annually in the fall (October). Donations are deductible to the extent allowed by law. Orders, subscriptions and donations can be made on-line at www.phantomdrift.org.

Phantom Drift
PO Box 31001
Portland, OR 97231

Phantom Drift accepts on-line submissions from January 1 – April 30.

AN INTRODUCTION TO *PHANTOM DRIFT* ISSUE SEVEN:

THE FANTASTIC AS A REFUSAL TO FALSIFY THE MYSTERIOUS

The truth is that my stories do not possess the slightest literary merit, the slightest effort. If some of them last, it will be because I received and transmitted what was latent in the depths of my psyche without losing too much, which comes from a certain experience in not falsifying the mysterious, keeping it as true as possible to its source, with its original tremor, its archetypal stammer.

—JULIO CORTAZAR, from *Around the Day in Eighty Worlds*

It is a severe pleasure to welcome you, one and all, to this seventh issue of *Phantom Drift*, a concoction of heretofore unknown yet potent proof which may just contain a Chupacabra or two—and an issue suitable for the warning-label, *contents may induce reverie—or even hallucination.*

We've titled our seventh literary child after a line of Pablo Neruda's: "My creatures are born of a long denial." For the priest, though commonly prescribed as a vatican-approved vanquisher of demons, is not the sole performer of exorcisms. As Julio Cortazar confesses elsewhere in his aforementioned essay, so, too, is the writer who traffics in the fantastic an exorcist:

> *An admirable line of Pablo Neruda's, "My creatures are born of a long denial," seems to me the best definition of writing as a kind of exorcism, casting off invading creatures by projecting them into universal existence... as if the author, wanting to rid himself of his creature as soon and as absolutely as possible, exorcises it the only way he can: by writing it.*

Cortazar's readers might first think of past literary "creatures born of a long denial"— of Shelley's Frankenstein, or Kafka's Gregor Samsa turned to a beetle, or perhaps, many characters who bear fates most unfortunate—say, Philomela, or Actaeon, from Ovid's *Metamorphoses*. These readers might even reflect upon future ramifications— inhumane phenomena born of human fallibility, improvident rapacity, and/or sheer carelessness—deforestation or global warming, for instance. As I write this, Hurricane

Irma, a category five hurricane likely spawned by global warming, threatens the Florida coast. The Indian Creek and Eagle Creek fires have merged to burn over 30,000 acres in the Columbia River Gorge—quite possibly due to a teenager's tossed firework.

We need to listen more carefully to these creatures, to learn lessons from them, to recover what survivors and small lives we have left. As Giles Goodland writes in "Witness," *Let's ruin the world less. At least / replace the dead with sadness, / thought. As a ghost departing an exorcism/ the moth flows behind.* As David Russomano's sphinx assures us in William-Carlos-Williams-esque fashion, *So much depends / on your answer.* Yes, there are many lessons, and much worthwhile terror and delight in these exorcisms, in our very own transmittals from the psyche and archetypal stammers. And many wonders in the creaturely contents, the furious little heartbeats in this cabinet of curiosities--our seventh trove of fiction and poetry which refuses to falsify the mysterious. Here are three of GennaRose Nethercott's 50 Beasts that Break your Heart. Here is, "curled on an ice floe" "in the arctic sea," Armin Tolentino's dragon with its "shattered wing." Here is Samantha Edmonds' looming, shadowy moonman and the stickmen of Alan Clark. Here is David Russomano's sphinx, posing its conundrums and stalking the menacing silence afterward with its "eagle eye" and "the poise of a lioness." Here is Tom Weller's tale of a pig whose squeal knocks out a narrator's teeth and inflicts him with a world's-record-setting fit of hiccups. Here are the "birds of paradise, the red monkeys and silver unicorns," illustrative inhabitants of Fiona Marshall's Borgesian labyrinth, "The Marvellous Book," a tome which sends its protagonist editor on a search from which "no one would rescue us, not even the church..." And Miranda Schmidt's shapeshifting husband in her story, "Familiar," who was "darling as a golden retriever," in a story whose narrator, as she wonders if "that metamorphic nature, that hint of uncertainty within" is "part of why she loved him in the first place," seems also to be speaking metafictionally of the exorcisms and transformations of the fantastic.

By now, you certainly must be anxious to read! But before you dare to traipse into such a shapeshifting bestiary, please allow me to qualify the "we" responsible for this enterprise, as a slightly altered editorship of *Phantom Drift* has chosen, captured, and framed the work in the issue before you now. I have newly assumed the duties of managing editor. For issue seven and presumably into the foreseeable future, David Memmott and Leslie What have agreed to share their considerable talents as contributing editors. Peter Grandbois and Martha Bayless remain steadfast beacons as fiction editors. Mary Bond, new to her post, and Ki Russell, are our poetry editors, having agreed to be like hummingbirds seeking the most select fabulist poetic nectars. Though in the future she will assume a consulting role, Sue Memmott saved us more than once once again with her fiscal practicality and genius. And Kristin Summers continued to do her unusually stunning work designing the journal.

Thank you, one and all, for your efforts in compiling and completing this impressive issue. Thank you to the contributors, for producing such memorable fabulism. Thank you, Alan Clark, for your splendid cover art. And thank you, readers, as always, for your support, for spreading the good word, and for reading *Phantom Drift*. I hope you will thoroughly enjoy your read.

Matt Schumacher
Managing Editor
Phantom Drift

TABLE OF CONTENTS

Introduction

🪢 FICTION

⬭ POETRY

☉ NON-FICTION/FEATURES

Fiona Marshall

THE MARVELLOUS BOOK

We, the Publisher, knew that there was such a book, but almost nothing more. The Manuscript was said to have existed in various forms throughout history, but what we wanted was the autographa, the original Work: created before the dawn of time on an island which had long since sunk beneath the waves. From the scraps extant, of which we had one, secured in the vaults of our library and named the Codex Marylebonus, we knew it was written on vellum in an unknown script from left to right, and that its language baffled all interpretation, whether it was hoax, glossolalia, or just some tongue too old to be understood. But as well as being of venerable antiquity, and reputedly crafted in the most marvellous calligraphy, with singularly beautiful, hand-painted illustrations, the Book had one feature that interested us primarily: it was said to be different every time it was read. That is, the words were not static on the page, but changed according to the mood and needs of the reader. It was said to speak directly to those who consulted it with such devastating pertinacity and intimacy that they were never quite the same afterwards; it could, literally, have been written for them. This private meaning was given in tones ranging from tender solicitude and comfort, to dry humour and, at times, brutal sarcasm. No wonder we were keen to acquire it. It was the industry dream, the one golden Book which made all others unnecessary. I speak, by the way, for a non-existent entity when I say 'we'; it is the 'we' of editors and royalty that I use. I may as well admit now that this was a personal quest.

Living alone as I do, in a tiny flat in that tortuous, labyrinthine London barracks the Barbican, a life made possible by a wall-bed that pulls down every evening for my urban repose, the search for the book took on more importance than it would have had I been, say, my elder brother, Ignatius. His quest was laid down earlier in life and was far more successful. With an annual income of £sterling 7 million, he lives comfortably in Kensington and New York, with his wife and three children. Such people do not exist, you will say, and I am tempted to agree. I sometimes doubt his existence even more than that of the Book. He impinges on my life far less. But I digress. I, who wear the sign of the Book on my forehead.

There was of course no question of tracking down the Author. A relief from our point of view, which is, roughly, that authors are a necessary evil. No tiresome lunches to stroke their ego, no crossing swords with agents. Authorship was safely anonymous; a collection of sages whose bones were scattered over desert sands that had once been seas. Copyright was also no problem of course. The difficulty lay in getting hold of the manuscript. Apart from the *reliquiae antiquae*, the few curled relics of ancient papyrus held by ourselves and one or two other publishers, there was no trace of the typescript. We didn't even have a title, let alone a contents page or synopsis. No one had any real idea whether it was a book of divination or of mystical secrets, a *mysteriorum liber* of revealed magic, or celestial wisdom sent to light poor mortals in a darkling world. Some people said it was one of seven, written before the creation; it was the Book of Atlantis, the original Akashic Records. It came from the angel Raziel, who revealed the Book of Secrets to Adam in the Garden of Eden; it was the Book used by Joseph, the great diviner, when he interpreted Pharoah's dream, and when he scryed from his cup. The manuscript had been buried with many charms and spells beneath the ruins of Machu Picchu or the Egyptian Sphinx.

All this was no use to us. As stated, the language was a mystery. Cryptographers and code-breakers were unable to decipher the 15 lines we held, or the two pages locked away in an American university, or the bundle of fragments said to be secreted somewhere in China. We didn't even know if the writing was good or bad, although as we have often observed, good writing is no guarantee of sales, while bad writing often sells quite well, particularly if it has a strong mythology in its favour. We were fully aware of the nonsense of a life-changing oracle written in a script unknown to living woman or man, but this only added to the Book's mystique, and with the blind optimism of our race we trusted in finding the right translator when the time came. In the last issue, lack of intelligibility never deterred any publisher bent on making a fortune from a book with such a potent reputation for being not so much magical as alive. Meanwhile, publishing truisms apart, all we knew for sure was that the manuscript had disappeared.

This alone kept our House going for many years, that great crumbling ruin on an island in the midst of the swirling London traffic. Dues on the Book, that is, advance orders, were immense, at one point close on a million. Shared fictions, like the belief in money, go a long way to sustain society. What else drives the stock market but the fiction of gold? Supported by bishops and royals and all others who deal in sacred story, we floated along for many years, a huge foundering hulk on the London tide, but even we could not remain indefinitely afloat upon rumour. The day eventually came when we were threatened with closure unless we actually published. The long corridors of the building echoed with consternation and in its enormous spaces we huddled in the kitchen, tucked away at the side on the ground floor. For decades every morning this small galley had sent out the scent of toast, drifting up the stairwell and all three floors of that cavernous old palace, here every morning indeed I consumed two slices of toast with marmalade myself before climbing the stairs to my office on the first floor, here every morning at 7.45am the oldest editorial assistant, who had been there for 28 years, could be seen making the Publisher's morning tea in a silver teapot and mug, carefully scuttling off with a tray into the dark recesses of the building. In the kitchen we celebrated birthdays and anniversaries with monotonous regularity and insistent cake; and, much more occasionally, leaving dos, usually preceding the leaver's decease by a short period. Here we exchanged gossip, compared books we had read, and even hinted at our innermost dreams that one day we would find the Book, leave this place and live our own lives. Now all this might be gone.

We had by no means been idle in our search for the Work. I had indeed devoted myself to the search while still an intern, had set out most willingly, leaving our comfortable offices, the armchairs and red cushions and paintings and shelves of bright spines, the tall windows onto the London plane trees with their seed balls bristled hard against a grey sky. I had travelled not to the ends of the earth but to the limits of my comfort zone certainly, as everyone must who leaves the London bubble; braved the crowds at dry and dusty antiquarian fairs, ransacked the storage drawers of obscure museums in rundown seaside towns, trodden in my town shoes down muddy Welsh lanes to converted barns crammed with books. And always the visits to authors, to their adobe homes at the top of blue cacti hills, to their inner, mad sanctums in universities and hospitals, to their studies of gloom in dystopian basements. As in a dream, I visited them all.

Returning not empty-handed—the vanity of authors made that impossible—but to note with increasing irony our motto, engraved on cornerstone of our building: *Except the Lord build the house*. Perhaps the manuscript was buried under that. It was a joke among us that the manuscript was in fact hidden somewhere on the premises, though I was the only one to take this seriously. On quiet rainy afternoons, when the London light was sallow and grey, I would go down to the stacks in the basement, that vast catacomb of battered folders, yellowing files, and paperbacks curling on the shelves, neglected by generations of editorial assistants who had far bigger aspirations than to catalogue such literary casualties. Long after my internship was over, and I had been promoted to editorial assistant, I continued the search, sifting through the rejections and the unholy machinations of the green ink brigade, which by and large merely foretold the imminent ending of the world and were uniformly dire. I would ponder such exhalations at lunchtimes as I walked the adjacent park where the roses each held a heartful of silver drops poised on the brink of rolling into each other. Beneath the clouds, dark grey and thunderous, people carried light umbrellas as if walking in a Japanese print, and every two minutes came the long summer sigh of a plane crossing the London skies.

It was part of my job as young editor to fend off the callers claiming to know the secret of the Book. These were many. They would mount the wide stone steps and turn up in the massive foyer with its twin staircases—this was in the days, which seem quite medieval now, before London offices locked their doors, of course. Mostly our callers were seedy, tight-eyed men from the provinces, passing through on their long pilgrimage of madness, with their one story and a briefcase stuffed full of evidence. We also had our regulars. The hobo Leon, for example, claimed to have the remnants of a quire among all the grey, tightly-tied carrier bags he trundled up and down the London roads in his supermarket trolley. He said it was written not on parchment but on living skin shed by the last god to leave Ithaca, the mythical island. It healed the sick, he said. In his multi-coloured woollen hat, he would stand in the foyer muttering, 'Bright island—fire island—' but he didn't know what he meant, nor even where he came from. He shook his head to every enquiry—Peru, Mexico, Guatemala. 'Too far,' was all he said. 'Too far.' Short and stocky, he looked like your archetypal, ubiquitous panpipe player and once indeed he did pull out some pipes and play: barely a tune but some wavering, quavering memory which floated up the stairs and brought the commissioning editors out like so many adult Hamelin children, faltering over the stairwell. As he breathed into the pipes I had the feeling I did know or ought to know where the Book was, I almost remembered where, but the memory sank back just as it was about to break surface. Once too I persuaded him to unpack and show me a corner of the manuscript. It was torn, scuffed yellowed paper which may once have been of good quality, with a few simple, faded pen strokes. *No puedo escribir*, he whispered; *no puedo leer*. He could not read.

Occasionally there would be signs, hints; reported finds in Russian monasteries, the supposed discovery of ten more pages in a library in Buenos Aires which later proved to be fake, a time capsule from 1698 containing a manuscript in old Catalan, found in Barcelona while digging an extension to the metro. A rumour of the Foreword, tracked down to some canny psychologist in north London who used the Book as a symbol of the Well, the collective unconscious, in a series of self-serving newspaper articles.

By the time I was senior editor, the Book was part of myself, irretrievable. Its influence, visionary, ironic, detached, permeated me while awake, and, when I slept, reams of bright letters would start falling from the ceiling like magical flowers. Passages of words danced in the darkness and illumined my whole life. I could see the illustrations, the golden birds of paradise, the red monkeys and silver unicorns, the exquisite plants unknown in this world, the thick and thin curvilinear letters that quavered sharp and black on the golden page. All night the words and the meaning were perfectly lucid, but in the mornings my grief was to remember only the visual images, not the meaning.

Only very gradually—I am ashamed to admit my naivety—did it come to me that there was no possibility of finding what I sought, only very slowly did I lose faith in the printed word. Not until I was Publisher did I understand that it was not for me to—I was not able to make the transition between the reality of the inner world and its written manifestation in the outer. I did not know that you do not find the Book; it finds you.

Now, huddled in the kitchen, we faced the fact that our search was over. We had had time enough to look. The 'Find the Book' campaign, diligently backed by our friends in the media, had brought in everything but what we sought. From the days when we typed everything out on Remingtons with carbon copies, to a slick web page and the senseless Twitter feed run by an intern or two, we had found nothing. Nothing but madness and lies. The building was falling into ruin; the vast roof leaked, we were losing half a million pounds a year. No one would rescue us, not even the Church, not even brother Ignatius, who had promptly turned down my hint that he might profitably invest some of his millions in us. No, he said; there was no Book; publishing was dead. Probably, he said, the Book was virtual in any case, existed in its bright entirety in the cloud, could be downloaded any day for free. These days all you needed to create a book was an ISBN and a meme.

He knew more about publishing than I did after a whole lifetime in the industry.

I slipped away from the gabbling crowd in the kitchen and out of the building into the park where the turgid London summer was in full sway. The trees were massive and dark green, as if they held rain; a few crinkled leaves had dropped early, fool's gold in this August circling like a great beast. Ignatius was right, the trustees and governing body were right; the Book had not found me, I had not succeeded in putting down what I saw into words. I had failed. It was time for those still in the kitchen to finish their cake and go up to their offices to start packing. The vast building would be sold for a song and converted into luxury flats, or used as a superior events venue. The rest of us would float, flotsam and jetsam on the London waters; the younger ones would get new jobs. I walked on, down the long avenue bisected by flower beds, through the rose garden and across the little bridge over the lake where ducks and herons were authentically themselves in the middle of this urban terrain. In my pocket I had the piece of vellum we had kept locked away for so many years and I fingered its soft, creamy texture as I walked. Everyone had forgotten it, the one scrap of evidence we had, of the real existence of the Book. This I had to weigh against a lifetime of failure and disbelief. Which was to win? Why not simply toss it into the lake, where the trees plunged in deep all round the sides? No one would miss it, no one look for it. I was Publisher; it was up to me to reject or accept such manuscripts and sad scraps of writing as came my way. Leaning on the fence over the lake, I took the vellum out of my pocket and looked at it; it was more faded than I remembered, the script less gorgeous; yet it had a yielding, flexible indestructible quality abut it, like skin. It was like some eternal simulacrum of one of the park roses, crumpled, soft, as it were wrapped around its own heart. If I did drop it into the lake, it would probably just float, like a rose on water. I realised it was not for me to throw away.

I turned away from the lake, to where the park stretched ahead, a wide parched path beside more rain-heavy trees. The bright Book was still there. Its unicorns and black pen strokes unchanged, untouched. I could see it still, its capital letters in red, its illustrations in medieval dull green and gold. It was speaking to me still, in that sage, ironic voice without words, a murmur as constant as the London traffic and as eternal. And its meaning I could almost grasp. Putting the vellum back in my pocket, I walked on, towards the north end of the park.

GennaRose Nethercott

THREE POEMS

from *50 Beasts to Break Your Heart*

LOORUS

Some people say the Loorus looks like a man. Others say a hare. Others compare it to stone or to a silver coin or a bowl of milk, filling and emptying and filling again. It hovers just above the horizon line, a nocturnal animal nibbling at the fatty dusk. When it grows thirsty, it tugs the tide towards its lips. It is easily insulted, so don't mess with it. Call it by a false name, and the Loorus will make all your exes call you on the same night. Yes, it has that power, and yes, it's that much of a jerk. In the ancient times, scholars worshiped it. They studied it through telescopes. They logged its movement across the sky in little notebooks. They didn't realize it was alive.

SPARK PANTHER

The Spark Panther can outrun its own soul— faster than its sorry prey, faster than sound, faster than the human eye. Its ghost, not so quick, topples out of its body into the dust. Soulless, the Spark Panther is a vicious hunter. It will rend the larynx from an antelope without remorse. It will gather enough meat to last several months, and then it will settle as it waits for its soul to catch up. Meanwhile, its soul begins the journey back to its host. Eventually, the spirit returns and the Spark Panther is made whole, again. If the soul arrives too quickly, before the Panther has had time to feed, the creature will be so overcome with guilt at the sight of its slaughtered prey that it will be unable to eat. It will paw at the mournful earth, burying the bodies, its belly empty.

NAWL

At the crest of its wet, dark, tentacles is a torso. At the peak of its torso is its head. Supporting its head is its throat. In the middle of the throat is a switch.

Switch it on, and the Nawl feels the way anyone feels. Its life, like any life, is a series of small griefs. Sweethearts come and the Nawl flickers awake, its many limbs blooming like lilacs. Sweethearts go and the Nawl writhes in the murk, remembering. Fear comes and the Nawl squeezes shut. Fear goes, and the Nawl unravels. Its heart swells and retreats, swells and retreats, swells and retreats again.

But when the little grievings grow too many, the Nawl flips the switch off. Then, it no longer feels anything. It floats silently in black pools filling with stormwater. It watches the sky, unmoved by the waxing and waning of the moon. It wants for nothing.

 DAVID RUSSOMANO

SPHINX

Before you go
any further and believe
everything
that they've told you
about me,

take the time
to ask yourself why
a true monstrosity,

something ravenous
with an eagle's eye
and the poise
of a lioness,

would ever postpone
a meal for a riddle

when she could
just as easily pounce,
throttle, swallow,
and be done with it?

Consider this
and your next words
carefully;

so much depends
on your answer.

 ## KATIE DIETER

ABYSMAL GIGANTISM

My husband takes my hand in his hand and my hand is so small.

My hand is not small because my husband's hand is so manly and large and it's not small because it is, on its own, such a small, feminine hand.

It's small because the fat suit, despite being state-of-the-art, ends at the wrists with cinched sleeves. Fat gloves are extra.

My husband fumbles for where I open. It's been months since I put on the fat suit and he's out of practice. Sometimes we joke that the fat suit is to keep him in shape but I never forget that it's for me, to remind me: at the very least, I am less fat than this. Even though I gently guide his hand to my pancaking left breast. Even though he lingers there, caresses.

From our neighbor's house comes a roaring clatter and a wrecking hurt of noise. It sounds like suitcases loaded with lead ball bearings are flying onto careening luggage belts. Our room rattles, and not with love. We can't figure out what they're doing next door. My husband thrusts and I listen for clues. They're building—something—that much is clear. But the problem is, what? We can't tell from the outside. Nothing's different. We can only hear it. Like our house is a stethoscope to our neighbors' ballooning house belly. To our neighbors' early stage colonial revival pregnancy.

It doesn't take long once he's inside of me. When I can feel he's close I say, baby, the ball bearings are popping all those suitcase zippers wide, wide open.

~

I was so tiny as a baby my father thought he might break me just by touching, by propping up my bottle with excessive force. My mother marveled at how she could hold me with just one arm, my head nestled snug in her upturned palm. I have always been extremely pale, and my newborn skin glistened like a windowpane. In pictures from those early days my face and hands and spaghetti noodle legs are all wrapped in bright blue cords of blood.

By the time I was one I was as big as a two-year-old. My only pants were elastic-banded leggings because nothing else could reach around my squishy mound of potbelly. All through elementary school I was mistaken for a short, pudgy teenager. At the swimming pool, splashing with other girls in the shallow end, one kick of my tree-trunk leg would unleash a tidal wave. Meanwhile, the other girls were free to slip under the water with a tiny burble, unnoticed.

Puberty, thankfully, was kind to me. I grew taller but not wider. By college, I was almost willowy. When I met my husband I tried to tell him, don't trust what you see. Also, don't look too close under the hood. Or maybe just, you're a fool if this fools you.

Fat settles and settles again. The world pools around my ankles. No matter where I look, I can't find the drain.

~

I stand up from the gathering bathwater and shake my hand. My sleeve is wet.

Cat shadows scurry past the open door.

When we adopted the cats from the Humane Society we had no idea how close to death by starvation they'd been until we gave them their first baths and all that wet hair pressed in against their soggy skeletons.

For this intrusion into their privacy, they scratched our arms to pieces.

I think I read it in the paper once, that a woman from North America moved to South America and waterproofed her apartment, filling it knee-deep with water like some kind of glorified kiddie pool. Then she carried a dolphin in, squirming and slippery from the sea. Her feet puffed up with wrinkles. The skin on her calves and her knees bulged, waterlogged loose from her heavy bones. She kept urging her dolphin up from the skin of the water, outside the water skin that held his dolphin skin. She gave him a name and he gave her one too; when he blew it from his blowhole she heard the clattering of so many stones.

I look down at myself, at my own skin and what it offers. From our neighbor's house comes a shattering and a wrenching twist of metal. I notice that my ankles are swelling. Soft and doughy, swaying slightly, I breathe to steady myself. The black and white geometry of the bathroom floor reassembles beneath me.

Finally, I take off my clothes.

~

When I check in for the appointment, the receptionists behind the desk eye me skeptically. I avoid their gaze and focus on the powdered low-cal soup packets and tiny, fruit-flavored snack bars displayed on the corner of the reception desk like some kind of figure-conscious animal's hoard.

The waiting room artwork is minimalist blue shades. There is not a single trashy magazine plastered with the trendy skeletons of famous people. I look through the glass door into the beige hallway with beige floor tiles at the scale that is a wide platform with tall handlebars.

This is not the right appointment, I know it is not, not for me, at least, but it is something to say. *Today I went to my appointment*. I am always at work on this issue. I have the urge to clutch the armrests of the waiting room chair but I am strangely off-center. The chairs have been carefully designed. They are one-and-a-half-seaters. The space between where my butt cheek ends and the left handlebar rises is immense.

I shouldn't be here. I know I shouldn't. This is beyond the scope of my struggle. I know it, but I don't feel it. A doctor in a crisp lab-coat and neat loafers appears in the hallway, behind the glass door. The plan is for me to cross the threshold and join her. I jump to my feet and rush out through the exit. I don't need the doctor to tell me I'm not seeing clearly. That's not what I need.

The doors, as I rush out, shrink me in their largesse. For the briefest of moments I am a slim, silvery minnow, and then I'm back on the other side.

~

I keep having visions. I want to say: not the crazy kind, where I see things that aren't real and go around like they're real and make poor life choices in the name of their realness—but what are visions if not visions?

I round the corner from the kitchen into our entryway and catch a glimpse of myself nine months pregnant, my belly beyond enormous, twin enormous, in the entryway mirror. I stop, clutch my midsection.

Of course I'm not pregnant.

Some days I wake up and absolutely none of my pants fit. I try to pull them on and they all get stuck somewhere midway up my thighs. I throw them off in disgust. I call in sick at work. My husband comes home and all my pants are having a wild pants party in a mound on the floor and I'm just sitting up in bed with a big shirt on.

Some days, my husband tells me back to myself. He says: Brown, glossy hair. Nice tits. A good waist and an ass worth grabbing. It's like he's a flatteringly skewed mirror in a department store dressing room. Other times, he just sighs, says, "Do we need to break out the fat suit again?" And then I go up to him and push my face into his neck, make the top of my head his chin rest.

~

My husband waits while I put on the fat suit. From the other room I can hear him tap out notes on the piano. The fat suit is of a piece, which makes sense once it's on, but it is utterly baffling when balled up and shapeless on the carpet in my bedroom. On the bedroom carpet that is a blush rose because it seemed like a good choice back when we had a choice. The balled up fat suit, mound of shed skin, on the blush rose carpet—it feels like I am about to put my naked body inside a murder victim.

I step in through the fat suit collar. I point my right toe and attempt to direct it straight down the leg hole but my foot pops out the right wrist hole, toes pointed and straining.

I peel my leg back out. By the time I slide my right leg through the right leg hole, my husband's piano plinkings have disintegrated into diatonic hops. My foot is pressed into the blush rose carpet, toes spread, defined by bones.

From the neighbor's house comes the metallic moaning of saws. It makes me shiver. From my thigh, the dangling fat suit wobbles, pink and wrinkled, a misplaced and overgrown wattle.

I rush to get my left leg in and once it's done I look down at myself, at how I'm bifurcated: fat suit on the bottom, self on top. I decide to sit down. The upper part of the fat suit, ballooning from my waist, knocks me off balance. My husband has stopped playing the piano. Next door there are two saws going now, maybe three.

If I don't pull the fat suit all the way up soon—right now—then the door will open, and in will come my husband. He will find me here.

He will find me here peeled, half out of my shell.

~

I approach my neighbor's house from the back, through a loose board in the fence.

A crescendo of staple gun or the sawdust screech of a ripped floorboard—hard to decipher from my neighboring distance—and I ran down the stairs and out the door.

Along the way, I just missed stepping in a pile of cat poop on one of the old towels we put out. My husband always says, I wonder if we stopped putting the towels out, if they'd stop doing it. That's as far as we ever get.

Inside the fence space, I try to calculate how much longer I'll fit here— mathematically, according to the rate of my expansion. But then I'm through and I still don't have the math right.

The neighbor's backyard is well kept, placid, ordinary. It provides no evidence.

I walk behind the back porch, lean over a prickly bush, and stand on my tiptoes. I peer in through the bottom third of a window, catching slivers of a room from between the slats of a venetian blind. I can't make a whole out of it and the construction sounds don't guide me.

As I walk back across the lawn and toward my own, I look up to my bedroom window. One of the cats is in there, now that I've left.

Bushy in the window; a self-satisfied silhouette.

If I were one of those people who gets off on calling pets horrible names, this would be the perfect moment. Instead, I suck my stomach in and turn sideways and even as the panic of not fitting through the fence overwhelms me, I slip through.

~

Afterward, always, my husband returns to the piano. He plays Debussy, or sometimes Liszt or Haydn, but I don't really know the difference. My body, in the fat suit, after sex, is mostly just my body. The only thing that keeps me separate from the hanging pouches of my fat suit is that I can feel the way it clings on the inside to my sweat, but every time I run my hand under the curve of my flapping fat suit arm, it comes up clean.

Sometimes I just turn on the ceiling fan and lie back flat on the bed with my arms out, breathing, watching what my chest does, what my stomach does, how I'm layered there.

Eventually I sit at the edge of the mattress with my feet swinging off and wrap my fingers around the nearly invisible edge of the fat suit collar. I hook my fingers there and pull. The suit's naturalistic stretch marks and cellulite wormholes morph. I watch them. I yank the suit down below my shoulders, past my lackluster under-breasts, until all I have to do is wiggle each arm up and out from the elbow. They pop free.

From here, I feel like a mermaid unfastening her tail. I'm going in reverse. Left leg first. The suit rubs; my under-skin is mottled pink and red. At the last second, I yank my left foot up and there's some kind of catch at the ankle and I trip and brace myself against the dresser. I look down.

Balled up fat suit, mound of shed skin, on the blush rose carpet. I have the urge to bury my face in it.

~

When I finally decide I've had enough, I march right over to the neighbor's house and ignore the knocker and knock with my knuckles straight on the wood of the door. My neighbor says, "Come in," like I might not be some nefarious stranger, some drug-addled interloper who's finally lost it.

The door is unlocked and it's only as I turn the knob that it occurs to me that waiting to confront my neighbor about the racket until it's been days since I've heard any racket may be ill-advised. But as soon as I step into the foyer, I can see that my concerns are beside the point.

My neighbor is in a two-piece swimsuit—blue with yellow daisies. I can't make sense of most of it at first, except to register that she's torn up all the old floors and replaced them with a light gray natural stone tiling, each tile ribbed in wavy streaks of orange and yellow. It looks like stone at the bottom of a river, dappled by sunlight.

My neighbor is up at the top of a—ladder?—positioned toward the rear wall of what used to be the living room. Her abs are surprisingly well-defined. The last time I saw her— months ago now—she was an attractive enough woman who went around in a little life preserver of chub.

"Just give me a sec," my neighbor says from the top of the ladder. I see now it is not really a ladder, but rather some kind of clear, acrylic staircase edged in glinting aluminum. She leans over and reaches into a large plastic tub and bobs up with some kind of fish flopping between her wrapped arms. The fish is a pink-orange with a weirdly purple eye that twirls around in its socket. It is as large as my neighbor's torso. She straightens, heaves her arms up and drops the fish into what I realize is the opening to the largest indoor aquarium I have ever seen. The fish sinks and then wriggles, starts in a direction, and is rapidly overtaken by the swirling tentacles of some giant skin-colored octopus, or squid, that darts out from a corner of the tank.

When I say darts out what I mean is: swiftly unfurls its mass of kite-string tentacles, kite-string tentacles long enough to wrap around the entire first floor of the neighbor's house. I step closer to the tank. The tank stretches feet and feet of blue-tinged glass above me. I press my face close and it gives off a coolness.

"I know," my neighbor says. "This part takes some getting used to." She reaches down to a lower step and scoops up a yellow beach towel, rubbing down her arms and ribby torso.

"I'm learning to accept it though. She will also eat smaller squid, like, squid that are smaller than she is, but I haven't been able to go for that yet, it just seems too . . . close." My neighbor turns the towel into a wrap and tucks it in under her armpits.

"I've been wondering," I say, searching for the right words. "About all this."

"Isn't she beautiful? Did you know they don't even know what causes it, the abyssal gigantism? Why squid like her and other fish that come from the deepest parts of the ocean get so large, I mean?"

I look back at the squid bobbing to the other end of the enormous, open aquarium that used to be several open, airy rooms.

"It could be pressure," my neighbor says, "All that ocean above them. Or some other kind of adaptation. There are theories, but the truth is, they're just theories. No one really knows."

I watch as my neighbor descends queen-like down the stairs.

~

Who doesn't want to live in a glass house? All those windows? All that looking out?

I say this to the cats. I'm making dinner and waving my spatula around like a conductor's baton, spattering oily drops. The nude wood cabinets are lightly freckled.

The cats slink back, shadows under the bottom lip of the island, the curve at the base of the cabinets. The pan is sputtering. I let it hiss.

It is now in vogue to imagine your glass house with an open floor plan so that yours is the most open open.

I swing my arms wide and the spatula strikes a metal cabinet knob, making a pleasant ding.

And if, as you should, you set your house down beside the sea, you may find yourself eating a light breakfast of salt-and-pepper-soft-boiled egg and simultaneously completely awash.

I drop two handfuls of pasta into the burbling pot and start to feel sick. The way the pasta went milky inside it, and how my face, in reflection, roiled.

This is the humanity of aquariums, the radical empathy required in the face of the world's would-be-thrown stones!

My eyes dart under the cabinets for flashes of cat's eyes.

Light? Your life would be loud with it.

I tap the side of the pasta pot with the wood spatula, cueing up percussives.

When I kick under the cabinets at the shadows, I discover the cats are all the way gone. They've left. Later I walk up the stairs and grow wispy, grow giant—lightheaded, woozy, loose-limbed, full of music.

~

Over dinner with my husband—clam linguine and a salad of dark greens with a lemony vinaigrette—I say, "I think they're finally done, the neighbors."

My husband sets his twirled forkful against the side of his clam linguine bowl. He pushes his thick, black plastic glasses frame back up to the bridge of his adorable crooked nose.

He smiles. His five o'clock shadow dips into his dimples. "Yeah? You might be right." Something comes to him and his smile grows wider. "I've really been savoring the quiet."

"Yeah," I say. "Yeah."

I don't know if I'm going to tell him. I wonder if he'll believe me. I stab around at my leafy greens. I pour more wine. The wine forms clots at the top of the glass, streaks down. I throw back a mouthful.

My husband sucks the noodles from his fork, fishes for another bite, says, "Will you put it on?"

"It?" I ask.

"You know," he says. He drains his wine. His teeth are slightly purple and there's a gummy chunk of clam squashed between two darkened teeth. "What if you were wearing it when I came home one day?"

I look at him.

"What if?" I say.

Once you go under the water, the water is over your head.

ARMIN TOLENTINO

TWO POEMS

DRAGON SCRIMSHAW

We meant to bring it home alive, the dragon
we found curled on an ice floe high in the Arctic Sea,
shattered wing, writhing. Its helpless weight
fixed to the ship's side. Offered it our rationed meat,
and, try as we did to rinse its yellow eyes of salt,
still it died. One harpooner plucked a tooth to scrimshaw.

Captain found out about the thieving scrimshander,
lashed his legs seven times while screaming that a dead dragon
was still worth more than a thousand barrels of oil; the salt
would preserve it. But we begged to cut it loose, let it sink into the sea.
Too heavy to tow and sharks were nipping chunks of meat
from its belly. But Captain said the corpse would pay its weight

in gold. We sailed home slowly, the extra weight
a burden. Without whaling, killed time with smoke and scrimshaw,
dreamt of women soaked in syrup and wine who would meet
us at port. In Spring, we crossed Cancer and the sky erupted as if the dragon
had breathed its doomed flames into the thunderclaps. The sea
churned black beneath us. The storm waged an assault,

the deck punished with rain until each man was swallowed by salt
water or stabbed by screws of lighting. Except me. The weight
of the first mate's body sheltered me until the heartbeat of the sea
slowed to stillness again. I drifted alone and began to scrimshaw
my daughter's name on teeth I pulled from the mouth of the dragon
to count each passing day. By thirty thousand, I'd run out of meat,

hardtack, and cod. I sliced the creature's back, cubes of scaly meat
I dried on the deck, old grey flesh packed hard with salt.
When, one day, I saw the sun eclipsed by a swarm of dragons
I understood I'd never see my home again. The weight
of their shadows smothered me as they crossed heaven. I scrimshawed
my questions to God on vertebrae as I drifted a borderless sea.

I've tossed out the spyglass because I know what I'll see:
blue on blue horizon, where sky and water meet.
I've burned the sails for soot to color my scrimshaw;
I never seem to run out of bones. I drink buckets of salt
water, but I never seem to run out of life. I wait
for nothing, and nothing comes, as the centuries drag on.

ADRIFT AT SEA BENEATH THE DRAGON'S WATCH

Draco, the dragon constellation, is circumpolar; it never sets
in the northern latitudes and is visible every night of the year.

Seal my mouth with paraffin,
 I've nothing left to say.
   No psalm, no chantey, no curse,
no confession. I've stripped
  my throat raw screaming rescue,
but the sea has replied the same:
  There is no home for you.

   If Earth were flat,
 I'd float off the edge
and fall away, waterfall of shattered droplets.
      Instead I circle the sea,
 asteroid held in orbit, no hope
    to be released.

I mark time, not by moon,
 but stars I've seen vanish
   since I began to drift.
  Lights that lived a million years
    have burned out in my lifetime.
 Ursa Major, Great Bear,
  skinned of her luminous fur.
Orion reduced to shoulder and hip.

   Only Draco remains complete:
 wings, skull, and backbone
stretching the night. Above my head,

heaven collapses, star by star. I wait and watch
as the world distills to water, salt,
wind, darkness, dragon,
and me.

 NILS MICHALS

HAVE YOU, DESPITE ALL YOUR CLEVER MACHINATIONS

Have you, despite all your clever machinations, ever been accidentally undone by something trivial, something plastic? *I have* said the man as he raised his hand in a field full of poppies. All the poppies rolled their one good eye, as if sensing evening. From under their lids some whispered *kiss-ass*. No one could listen to one more Siddhartha story, no one cared about the summer the fjordhorse double-nickled bull haulers cross-country. But there he was, the man, ditzing on and on about some missing knickknack Napoleon and his horse. Of course, by this time the woman had ridden her beast into sawdust and the town was so used to her bare breasts, now completely nut-brown from summer, that her body was simply one more feature among many in a landscape: tree, rock, curvature of dune. Turns out the missing Napoleon had been moonlighting as a cake topper for some extra cheddar on the side. *Who could even know such a thing?* said the private investigator. *I could* said the man. The field groaned. Some of the poppies decided to just get faded on themselves. Some joined a look-sultry-and-absentmindedly-finger-your-little-hairs contest. Others, having had enough, unionized. And the horse? When asked about him, bric-a-brac Napoleon shrugged and said *one minute he was there, the next...nothing, just some hoof prints in pink frosting.*

 Tom Weller

SQUEAL

Hiccoughing
The longest record attack of hiccoughs was that afflicting Charles Osborne (b. 1894) of Anthon, Iowa, from 1922 to date. He contracted it when slaughtering a hog. His first wife left him and he is unable to keep in his false teeth.
—Guinness Book of World Records, 1978

There will be blood, warm as your morning coffee. But first there is the squeal. It starts before blade even touches flesh. Pigs know when death is near.

The pig hangs from the killing tree upside down, wiggles and thrashes and squeals, fighting against the hemp rope looped around his rear hooves, cursing the future. The pig's head hangs at your eye level, comes closer and then retreats with each desperate twitch, comes closer and then retreats as if considering a kiss, an attempt at seduction. But it's the squeal that's got you. The squeal is part weedwacker buzz and part diesel engine rumble. It is your mother's wailing the first time you broke her heart and the throaty commands of your red-faced father. The squeal grabs your spinal cord with two hands and shakes.

Above the two of you, the late-fall canopy of the killing tree is a riot of reds and oranges, a thing on fire.

You take up your knife, the knife that's as long as your forearm, the knife that feels like a sword, heavy and hungry for blood. The pig's squeal rattles your spine. You put your knife to the pig's throat.

You speak to the pig, speak words enveloped by the pig's squeal, words simple and heartfelt: *Thank you.* This you owe the pig. This is respect.

You drive knife blade through skin, through fat, through twitching muscles, through pulsing veins, through trachea. You witness blood and breath and squeal abandon pig, life rushing out of pig the way air exits a balloon.

You place an old coffee can under the pig to catch the rushing blood. Waste not. This, too, is respect. You feel the absence of the squeal. You feel the whole world around you changed.

You feel a pressure in your throat, a feeling like a tiny swirling storm has entered you, a feeling like that storm is growing, skies darkening, thunderheads building. You open your mouth to relieve that pressure. You hear the pig's death squeal erupt from your throat. You feel the world shrinking around you. You feel your spine shake.

This first squeal is all power, part trumpet's call, part right cross, part hurricane wind, part wrecking-ball swing, part shotgun blast. This first squeal steals from you, brazen, steals the air from your lungs, the moisture from your tongue, takes the teeth from your mouth and flings them into the greying light of the gathering dusk. You watch your teeth leaving you, a Cheshire cat smile exploded and tumbling through space.

One throat, two voices. One voice angry, scared, human, a rush of *shit*s and *fuck*s and *cocksucker*s, a thrumming flock of *God damn*s. This is the voice you long to hear, pray to hear even while you *God damn*.

One voice angry, scared, dying, porcine, a squeal that shakes your spine even as it escapes your throat. This is the voice you hear.

You want to bury the dying pig's squeal. You feel the squeal roaring up your throat, feel it lunging toward the light, feel it clawing, desperate to be out in the world. But as it crosses your bloody gums, your lips, the boundary lines that mark where you stop and the world begins, you swallow.

Swallowing the dying pig's squeal feels like how you imagine drowning must feel. You feel a weight in your chest, a tightening, feel as if suddenly your rib cage is one size too small. You feel tingling in the tips of your fingers, tips of your toes, even the top of your head. The top of your head crackles and sparks like an electric fire.

Hiccup. It bursts out of you, sudden, like a dragonfly, involuntary, like a blink, welcome as a kiss.

Hiccup. Hiccup. Hiccup. Hiccup, persistent as the laughter of children, quicker than a pig's squeal. You now know what the future will bring, can see it spreading out before you like an ocean on the horizon.

You won't stop hiccupping.

You will reach under the dangling pig carcass, pick up the old coffee can half filled with blood. You will pet the pig carcass on the head, scratch it under the chin. You will think the carcass looks so much like a boxer's heavy bag. You will leave the pig carcass behind.

You won't stop hiccupping.

You will walk back to the house, back to your lover. You will find your lover, back turned toward you, in the kitchen. Your lover will be busy, washing dishes or peeling potatoes. Your lover's hands will be fluttering through the air like two nervous sparrows. You will hiccup and those hands will still. Your lover will turn toward you, see your mouth, toothless and bloodstained. Your lover's eyes will grow big as fists, and your lover will ask, "What happened?"

Hiccup. You will set the coffee can half-filled with this pig's blood on the kitchen counter, a sound like the fall of a gavel. *Hiccup.*

"Try a deep breath. Tell me what happened."

You will dip your right index finger in the pig's blood. You will show the pig's ghost you will not be silenced. You will start to write on the kitchen counter, blood streak letters, red darkening to brown, your printing as precise as surgery. In pig's blood all over your home, you will write for your lover. You will write your story. You will write this story. You will write of death and respect and karma and revenge and choking on the voice of spirits. You will write of the feel of a pig's squeal. And you won't stop hiccupping, and you will keep writing, as long as your lover will have you.

# LINDSEY MARTIN-BOWEN

SILENT CANOPY
In memory of James Tate (December 8, 1943–July 8, 2015)

Under Caribbean skies, a penguin leads his brood
through tall grasses where cockatiels fly and alight
on branches. The arctic birds dart around snakes

and perform poisonous dances and gymnastics
in jagged steps, toes turned inward, whirling
away from vipers until the birds keel over.

Most penguins don't dig this hot aquatic scene
with thick palms instead of evergreens under skies
flat as blue paint inside a Victorian canopy for a royal

wedding. And smells of poi and hot spices don't do
their bills justice. They prefer salmon from icy seas,
where they swim and dive deep—far from a glowering sun.

Tonight, they'll try not to stink when they soak their feet
in Epson-salt water, sip a pear drink, and seek out a sailor
to help them find a ball of cheese, the perfect ball of Cheese.

HOLLY BURDORFF

NOW YOU WILL NEVER BE LOST

In this land of houseplants & pepper. In this realm
of snowballs & gold mines. Hereupon you travel
seven long yobs, seeking Croaky all the way. Lots
of frogs in tales like these. Lots of forests, too.
At the altar of the looking-globes you come

to a great fountain. The swarming locals
murmur *Welcome, lost far.* You do not correct them.
They bring you warm drinks. They try to make a photo,
but the flashcubes grow larger & larger, make quick
moves to swallow you whole. It is time to go
again. Now the lady-killer has picked up your trail
once more, follows along on her skull-furnace
sled, regurgitates your childhood swellings, LOUD,
for all passing travelers to hear. Now you've come
to the lake, where the loveliest larvae

sulk like boiled spleens. Do not eat a thing here.
One knocked tooth would break the charm and
cul-de-sac this whole land. The lady-killer is
always ten lengths behind you. The lady-killer lobs
placentas like grenades. *Cross criss cross*, hisses
the grass as it snuggles your toes. You swim
across, leave the lady-killer alone to weep. Ugly
lungbird. You pass a snowman farm & gnaw down
their fence. They screech their panic & you sing
them a ballad of free-range joy. The chillies
unruffle & knock towards the norths. So

do you. You're home again. In the kitchen, Croaky
whips fresh breakfast drinks. You rise your face.
Your faucet croons hello.

 ## LYLE ROEBUCK

THE CRAB

They handle death differently in the South—soften it up with slow speech or shoo it like a horsefly threatening to sting, which is not to say this is better or worse than how they cope in other places, just that it's different.

But it's summertime, when death is not much on anyone's mind and horseflies are a legitimate nuisance, and Mattie is eager to run down to the marsh to play with the other girls, Shell and Iris. There's a long wooden pier that angles like a broken leg one hundred yards through mud and tall grass to a river that doesn't flow so much as it rises and falls with tides. The marsh is more fun for the girls than the shallow pools of water between houses or tracts of undeveloped woodland where the only living creatures are ants, songbirds, and snakes. In the marsh, there is an assortment of life: rabbits, strange white birds that look like they've been folded out of paper, small dark hens, gators, and crabs—both fiddler and blue.

Except for Mrs. Dismuke, who is said to feed loaves of white bread daily to a large gator that comes to sun in her backyard, Ruthie has neither seen one nor heard of anyone seeing one, and Ruthie has lived by the water all her life. Gator sightings, as she understands it, are the purview of those with backyard swimming pools or small dogs. In her mind, the danger is the dock itself. It is in poor repair—rickety, rotting beneath, and missing planks (and that had been its condition years ago, the last time she had been to the end).

"You walk to the end!" Ruthie hollers from the belly of a recliner where she is stranded by her weight. "Don't run!" Ruthie doesn't have to guess—she knows where her granddaughter is going. To Mattie, her grandmother is Mee-Maw and always will be.

But the girl is already running, a jellied mass of chicken gizzards, necks, and backs spotting a pink trail from one corner of a Butternut Bread bag. Mattie brings the bait, Shell the traps, and Iris just herself. This is how it works. Although she didn't ask if she could have the chicken, Mattie can't imagine Mee-Maw will object, especially when she comes home with a cooler full of crabs for supper. Mattie imagines herself in this way—larger than life, like some kind of hero.

The midday heat is archetypal, the bayou's best impression of hell where white light squints the eyes from a sky so full of sun that the only relief is to keep one's gaze to the ground. By nine thirty, Mattie and Iris are standing at the cusp of lawn and marsh with the Devonshire estate to their backs.

"You got the traps?" Mattie asks. The blood soup has drained away and only flaps of yellow fat and violet bone remain, which she displays to suggest they need a trap more than they need Shell. Even as she asks, Mattie knows that Iris will say "No ma'am." Iris is black and poor, poor like Mattie, but somehow (and in ways she can't explain) it's better to be white and poor than black and poor.

Mattie would never say "No ma'am" to Iris.

"We gots to have a trap?" Iris asks.

"Yeah, dummy!"

But they don't have twine either. Shell is supposed to bring that, too, so Iris says nothing and sits beside Mattie on an oyster bed. And they wait.

Without saying anything, Ruthie curses Tom for skipping work. They can't afford indulgences, and although she stops short of calling it an indulgence to attend a funeral, the result is the same.

"I was the only white person there," Tom says. "Sat in back." These were as many words as he had said to his wife in days.

"Was there many people?"

"Yep."

Ruthie moves her head as a prelude to getting up, which is not going to happen.

"One of 'em, I think it was the sister, threw herself on the body whilst the casket was still open," Tom says. Ruthie does not want to interrupt, lest the miraculous speech stop.

"That right?"

"It was quite a show." Tom opens a can of beer. "I have to say, it weren't what I expected. That's the thing about death. You don't get what you expect."

Ruthie wouldn't have moved even if she could have. Struck by this odd, philosophical brush, she wonders if Tom stopped for a beer at Twin Oaks on his way home or if this man is some kind of imposter. If he keeps on like this, Ruthie decides she'll refrain from mentioning he can still earn a half-day's pay if he goes to work.

"What'd she die of?"

"Cancer," Tom says, downing half the can.

"The crab," his wife murmurs.

"Stomach, I believe."

She shudders to hear this. Ruthie cannot explain why, but ever since she was a girl and most impressionable to statistics (someone had told her once that one in four people will die of cancer), she has been sure that this would be her fate. Every occurrence in another person, known or not, terminal or not, is a harbinger of her own death.

"It was good of you to go," she says. "She reared you and your sister, after all. Even if she did get paid. God knows I ain't gettin' paid to bring up this one." Ruthie is thinking of her granddaughter, robbing the marsh and the neighbors of their lot.

"Where's she at?" Tom asks.

"Crabbin'," Ruthie says.

"Again? There won't be a crab left in Terrebonne Parish by the time school starts." Tom sits up and leans forward. "She ain't at the Devonshire place, is she?"

"Didn't say she wasn't."

"Damn. I hate that," he says. "What if they come back and decide to use their dock, and them girls is down there? Anything wrong'll be our fault."

"Easy to blame the poor," Ruthie says absently, and her lips begin to twitch as she spots the remote, which has fallen to the floor.

"I'm goin' to work," he says, swilling the rest of the beer.

"Drunk?" Ruthie says, and although she immediately regrets such discouragement, Tom is not fazed. On the way out, he bends over, retrieves the remote, and places it on the TV tray near his wife—as one would furnish a dog with its bone. She had not asked for it and yet she is grateful. He can read it in the way her lips are still.

Their bodies are like jewels fresh from the mine, but better than jewels because they move. Metallic blue foil backs with bright cayenne claws dotted in pearl teeth, the promise of a pinch worse than the reality. Even though Shell brings the traps, Mattie insists on being the one to hoist them to the surface. It's her bait, she reminds the other two. And, besides, this is her spot.

It is a magical moment to draw the weight against the resistance of dark water, when the O-framed basket clears the surface and there's a crab or two or three leeching to the carcass bait. Iris is appointed to overturn the traps into the cooler. If someone is going to get pinched, it's probably going to happen during this transfer. Occasionally one will fall short and launch itself from the end of the dock into the safety of the river. When this happens it's convenient to blame Iris, and the loss is subtracted from her total.

The afternoon can pass slowly on a dock. As the tide rises, the prospect of more crabs dims. Low tide gives the best luck, and the girls are aware of how shallow the river is when the waterline has receded the full six feet from the platform, exposing mounds of soft mud on both sides of a ford that's plugged with marsh grass and pocked with holes bored by fiddler crabs.

"I gots t' pee," Shell proclaims before disappearing to the shore. When she returns, trotting down the planks, she's cradling a rock.

Iris spots her first, wobbling toward the left side of the pier and then overcorrecting and nearly falling off the right. She stops short, six inches from the edge, and the missile plummets. It barely clears the end of the dock before plunging through ductile mud and out of sight at the river's edge. There's a wake as water fills the void. Fifteen feet away, two herons loll into a jade sky.

"Way to go, dummy," Mattie snaps. "Way to scare the crabs!"

"What's left of 'em," Iris says.

The fact is Mattie's last four pulls have come up empty, and most of the bait has been scavenged away.

"Whaddaya care?" Shell says. "'Sides, tide's comin' in."

"But we only got nine!" Mattie feels like crying, though more from rage than disappointment. "Nine ain't enough! That's only five for me and that ain't enough to stuff a snail!" The other girls don't question her math.

"That's okay, cheater," Shell says, turning back down the dock. "You can have mine. I'm tired. I'm goin' home."

––––––––––––

"Mee-Maw, I done caught eight!" the girl screeches, circumnavigating the yard's many obstacles: car tires, a bicycle frame, a couch, a box spring, and assorted wheeled toys. Ruthie is on her feet, limping to the door to meet her granddaughter.

"My stars, child. Eight what?" Ruthie already has a five-gallon pot on a burner out back. "Crabs?"

Mattie remembers that she forgot to ask permission for the bait—or to go in the first place—and puts on a sad look to compensate for whatever mercy a few crabs might buy.

"What's y'all gonna eat? I know," Ruthie cajoles. "You and Tom can have that leftover chicken." She finds it hard to be angry with the girl. As much as she despises Mattie's mother, her own daughter, Ruthie tries to adore her granddaughter as if she is a kind of second chance. "Let's get a look."

"They's big, Mee-Maw," the child says. When the cooler's lid is removed, there comes an uninspired scuttle toward the top. The crabs are the color of dirt, more bronze than blue. Having been out of the marsh for hours, the color of their claws has turned from pink to brown.

"There's nothin' to 'em," Mee-Maw says. "Put the lid back on. I've got a pot out back. I guess it's enough if I fix cornbread. I swear, child, y'all have crabbed that marsh to extinction."

At the mention of a pot, Mattie understands that all is right with the world—that Mee-Maw must have known where she was and that she does not care. And for Mattie, the pot is the best part. The cooler feels lighter as she shuffles barefoot over the kitchen's scored linoleum, curling along its seams like parchment. On the back stoop a pot is waiting, wide enough at its base to eclipse the gas burner below. The water is at a rolling boil, so furious that Mattie cannot see the bottom.

The crabs look like samurai, with daggers for eyes flitting in and out of russet shells while bubbles of air cluster around their mouths. In the failing daylight, they do seem smaller than they had on the dock, Mattie thinks. Mee-Maw follows her through the kitchen, stopping at the cupboard to bring out some cornmeal and grease.

"Here y'all go," the girl says, like she is doing the crabs a grand favor when she tips the cooler and causes them to tumble by their own weight into the pot. Suddenly the water is still—but the crabs are not still. Rather, they go insane with trauma.

Ruthie watches her granddaughter from her side of a gnarly screen. It does not bother her that Mattie went crabbing without permission, or that she helped herself to the chicken without asking, or that she might even have been mean to the other girls and bullied them out of their share of the catch. But it bothers her that Mattie is not afraid of this part, the part that should be hardest. Even the boys Ruthie knew growing up shied away at the end. But not Mattie. When the time comes to deal the crabs into the pot, there is no holding her back.

———————

"Mattie, you is Queen of the Crabs," Tom says, wiping his mouth and popping the tab on another beer. The girl's face glows. She loves attention, loves her grandpa, and invites greater praise.

"Mee-Maw says I crab too much. Says there won't be no crabs left."

Ruthie holds her tongue. It is all she can do not to make it known Tom had said this first. Somehow, Ruthie always comes out on the short end of the stick.

Because it's hot, they sit on the front porch where patched screens are barely enough to keep them from being eaten alive by mosquitoes. By eight thirty, the sun has set behind their shanty and the buzz of cicadas from surrounding woods ratchets up. In the space of one beautiful hour, the tops of pines fade from green, to rose, to violet.

"I'll tell ya what we'll do," Tom says, moved by the creative force of the beer. "Gather up all them claws!"

"What claws?"

"The crab claws, silly!"

"They's been throwed out."

"It don't matter."

"Tom—" Ruthie tries to intercede from the couch, though despite her enormous presence, she has no say and Tom shushes her with a wave of his hand.

"I'll get 'em out the trash! What're we gonna do?"

"We'll clean 'em up, bleach 'em 'til they's white as stars, then we'll make ya a crown with pinchers runnin' all around the outside. You think you'll have enough?"

"Stink up creation!" Ruthie wheezes.

"Don't pay her no mind," Tom says. "She's just sore 'cause she can't be Queen."

"Who gets to stay here all day and smell it? Not you. Not Her Highness!"

"If there ain't enough, I know where we can get more," the girl shrills— cautious in her exuberance not to mention the Devonshire place by name.

"Lord, if we don't already owe these crabs a heavenly debt." Ruthie is at her wit's end, giving it all she's got to stand.

"Run on," Tom says, "and fetch them claws."

To the west, the wind kicks up. Through the pines comes thunder. For several minutes, neither Tom nor Ruthie speaks. He drinks, and she broods. Then, as if on cue, lightning fractures the sky and the rain starts, first in drops that are easy to count and then in floods of sound like static.

"I don't know why you insist on makin' my life so hard," she says.

"Trouble with you is you don't know how to have no fun." The temperature drops, and all hell breaks loose—hail and a torrent that sprays in waves across the roof.

"And who gets to stay here all day to smell it? Not you. Not Mattie—"

"On second thought, I might be wrong," Tom says. Mists of cold rain hiss through the shoddy screens. He stands up, offering a hand to Ruthie. "Maybe you is Queen of the Crabs."

It rains non-stop for three days, and Mattie's mood worsens by the hour. "It's only water! Water never killed nobody!"

The girl is a terror, and Ruthie would just as soon get her out of the house as there, with the sinister band of claws balanced on her head and a smell like rotten fish trailing behind.

"Prisoner in my own home," Ruthie moans.

"That's 'cause you's so fat," the girl says. She knows Mee-Maw can't chase her.

But Mattie's glory is incomplete—her crown like a smile with teeth missing—and there is only one place to go to complete the mission.

By Tuesday afternoon the rain tapers off, and Mattie calls Shell and tells her to meet her at the dock.

"Can I go now?" Mattie tries one last time.

"No, child! How many times I gotta tell you. It ain't our dock." The girl sees why Mee-Maw is cross—the television remote is on the floor beside her ankle, which is the size and texture of a cantaloupe. Mattie picks up the device and places it on the table with deference. It is behavior, the girl concedes, not befitting royalty.

"What do you say?" Mattie asks.

"What I say is if you go to the Devonshire place, I will get out of this chair and I will whip the daylights out of you!"

For the half mile that runs from the shanties through woods to the marsh's edge, small kettles of low ground connect in soft pools of water. They make for patterns that skew the once familiar landscape, so it takes Mattie an extra few minutes to arrive at the Devonshire estate. As she makes it around back and discovers Shell is not there, Mattie begins to stew. A few minutes later, the sky spoils and the rain resumes.

In all directions, the marsh is bloated with the tide and rain. The water level creeps up, licking the good grass at the foot of the yard. Farther out, vast, swirling fields of gray water bury the patches of reed that usually outline tributaries. All is sea. Even with no way to track time, Mattie decides to wait for Shell. A minute later, she gives up. The cardboard frame of her crown, worse than being incomplete, is waterlogged and slipping from her brow.

Irritated as much with Mee-Maw as with Shell, Mattie turns and nearly runs into her friend. The girls' hair is lacquered to their heads.

"Nice hat," Shell says, trapless and without so much as a ball of twine. Mattie's crown slips to the tip of her nose then around her neck like a noose. A bag of hearts, the least part of the fowl, sags hopelessly toward the ground.

Thunder drones beyond the horizon, past fetid marsh and out over the gulf. The air is warm, moist, and uncommonly pleasant.

"I came for crabs and I ain't leaving without crabs."

Shell watches as Mattie turns toward the dock, now little more than a footpath.

"I only gotta have two more," she yells back.

"You ain't gonna catch nothin'," Shell says, following anyway. The planks are green with mold, and water bobs up between them. Walking is more like balancing on a raft. Reeds litter the way—evidence that the tide has recently been above boards, and on both sides of the dock the currents churn in broad eddies.

"You ain't gonna catch nothin'," Shell says again, but Mattie is too far ahead.

At the end of the channel, where the pier widens to a square platform, the river has risen seven feet, distended to the very lip of the dock. Mattie has ever seen the water so high or fast. The air is thick and cold, and Mattie takes off her crown and puts it at her feet between them.

"What if we can't get back?" Shell asks, but already Mattie is removing her shoes, ready to take a seat and let her legs dangle in the rushing, black water.

"What do you mean?"

"What if the dock washes away?"

It's not like Shell to worry, and this makes Mattie bolder.

"I guess we'll be stuck out here. Put your feet in." Shell, adapting to the new role of subject, takes off her shoes. "Or maybe we'll get swept away," Mattie says. "Lots of stuff *could* happen."

Shell dunks her legs into the water, and the current jerks her calves toward the river bend, pulling her fanny forward. "Whoa!" she gasps as her hands slam against the surface.

"Or maybe we'll die!"

"Maybe," Mattie says. "But I don't think so."

"Why not?"

"Because I'm Queen of the Crabs." Mattie offers this insight with great humility—onerously, as she reclaims her crown to inspect it for damage. "That's why."

"Who made you the queen of anything?"

To the east, beyond where the marsh ends and the gulf begins, a new blackness claims the horizon, broken every few minutes by the faint flicker of a lightning field. It's getting late and, with the weather, hard to tell how long before dark.

"I have an idea," Mattie says, her face as brooding as the sky. She knows she won't get what she came for, and because she is not used to being denied, someone must be punished. Mattie puts on the crown, as if to summon both the courage and the authority it brings. "Here's what I want you to do."

———————————

"Mattie's done fell in!" Shell screams with what feels like her last breath. She's run the entire way back only to find Ruthie on her feet—not what she had been told to expect—frying a skillet of okra for dinner. *"Down at the end,"* she gasps, full of drama, before collapsing onto the floor.

———————————

Fifteen years later, Mattie is home for her grandfather's funeral. It's winter, but the Devonshires are not at home. A maid answers the door and consents to the young woman going out back, where Mattie is struck by how nothing much has changed. She shudders to be in the same place, under the pergola where she hid as a child, seeing the marsh.

Nothing will ever change.

Color is siphoned from the sky, and from the side of the house Mee-Maw appears as an apparition plodding for the dock. The girl hardly knew her grandmother could walk, let alone run, and by the time Mattie makes it to the end of the yard, Mee-Maw is already halfway down the jetty.

But now Mattie walks slowly, knowing how the vision ends. It's the dream that haunts her in the city, where the crabs are always with her—the great survivor crabs, her subjects, coming back again and again on menus, in cartoons, and on advertisements to remind her who wins in the end.

At the edge of the dock, Mee-Maw would have seen the crown she'd left, but when the young woman arrives only the jagged teeth of shorn planks remain, now as then, and a long fall to the bank, and the river, and a life abundant, always there just beneath the surface.

 NATE PRITTS

WARRIOR

Pine surrounds the house
Each silhouette linked
                    By the darkness held inside
Anyone looking
        Might lose themselves
                    Might forget what makes the world
And in so doing   Lose their way back

I radiate out
        In attuned posture
                        And remember everything
The science of light
The fact that we die
That we have left ourselves open   To brutal conquest
But we each are warriors
        Are weapons   That need only to be aimed

The distant moon
        Tries to keep its light from your hair
But fails   Becomes intertwined
Becomes part of the scene
                            A technical incantation
Tries to brighten the interior resonance
Of your eyes
                I don't know when this is happening
Or where my power has fled
                It might not matter

I grab at two feathers   Dash them against the rocks
    That surround me

               They cannot help me

A glimmer in the nous
Even ethereal memory emanation   All have value
An intensity

But I am a warrior   And some battles
    Must be fought alone   And forevermore

Separate instances of snow
           Punctuate the yard
   Every so often
             You hear the wind

And then you don't hear it

Sometimes the morning light gathers
    Between heavy masses of cloud
        Before it streams out

And the only person on the street
               At this apocalyptic hour
Disconnected from anyone or anything else
Feels this new moment
             Rife with possibility

Everything is emptied of the regular motions

Sometimes I think I could stop breathing

Let my body die   And all my dark power fossilize
                        Over the long millennia
    To become a new planet
A caring home for a loving people

But every bird in the sky is haunted by the presence
              Of every previous bird
I stare at each one   Into it
Willing it to land or to take me

 GILES GOODLAND

WITNESS

The milled edge of a millipede
quicksilvers from under a
raised stone. It was coined
at point of decay. In the garden,
the bramble's blossom
the only thing almost still
visible. Cloud runs out of steam.
Through a thousand litres of fog
a moon the width of an eyelash.

Remove the clouds and we get
the lightning-print, struck
eye-vein, bare of anything
but structure. There are stairs above
the stairs and a sky partly
revealed, behind this one. But who are
the bound figures in the foreground?
Piranesi imprisoned his viewers
inside the lattice: struts
and stairwells, higher domes, towers.
Where shadows gather is an open gate
and an easy walk out, if we were
not bound by what we saw.

Let's ruin the world less. At least
replace the dead with sadness,
thought. As a ghost departing an exorcism,
the moth flows behind.

 J. J. ROTH

LUCKY SHANGHAI DUMPLING

I. The Disappearance of Hope

In the long-shuttered train station's parking lot, where food trucks often congregated to fill the needs and bellies of office park workers, high school students, and other hungry Silicon Valley lunch-goers, the Lucky Shanghai Dumpling truck became a fixture in a dual sense.

The first sense in which the truck became a fixture:

For several years, the plain, silver truck occupied the same space, day in and day out—often, though not always, between the stylized, silent, pink-and-brown Precious Cupcakes van and the garish, mustard-and-olive Bedouin Gyro and Falafel, Fetty Wap thumping from its back-counter boom box. The line for Lucky Shanghai Dumpling eclipsed those of the other ten frequently-appearing food trucks. It snaked through the parking lot, down several blocks of shadeless sidewalk, and into a cool, shade-mottled oak grove abutting a multi-building research facility.

What accounted for this humble eatery's wild popularity? Why did high powered executives, owners of modest green groceries or liquor stores, cashiers at Walgreens, college staff, retirees, recently laid off information technology workers, and homeless people who managed to scrape together enough coins for an order of dumplings, queue for hours just for a chance to spread their money on the counter?

The second sense in which the truck became a fixture:

Folklore.

It was said:

If you wrote a wish down, dropped it into the business card raffle fishbowl on the Lucky Shanghai Dumpling counter, bought your dumplings and ate them, something magical could happen.

The dumplings granted wishes, but not all wishes.

No one knew why some wishes were granted and others weren't, not even the two Nigerian college students who served dumplings out of the Lucky Shanghai Dumpling truck. Not even the people who cooked the dumplings, who no one ever saw. Not even the company that owned the Lucky Shanghai Dumpling truck. Not even the company that owned the company that owned the Lucky Shanghai Dumpling truck.

Or anyone else, for that matter.

It was also said:

God granted the wishes. Fairies granted the wishes. An ancient and immortal Chinese/ Egyptian/Brazilian/Native-American/fill-in-the-blank-sorcerer/mystic/shaman/fill-in-the-blank granted the wishes.

Aliens granted the wishes. A chemical leak from the multi-building research facility near the oak grove caused an aberration that granted the wishes. Cosmic radiation from solar flares caused an aberration that granted the wishes.

A random force in the universe that had become far less random because of the concerted mental energies of people wishing on dumplings granted the wishes. No one granted the wishes, people just believed the wishes would be granted, and karma rewarded that positive energy.

Then, one day, the truck failed to appear.

It was never seen again.

In its place stood the clear glass fishbowl stuffed with paper slips, dog-eared cards and waxy wrappings straining to break from their crystalline confines and sail away on the wind.

II. Some of the Materials

A business card, black block print on unimpressive white card stock, with a stylized tree against which a rake and shovel leaned, handwriting in pencil on the back, in Spanish.

Half a red and white Tootsie Pop wrapper, childish writing in black Sharpie, several misspellings and crossed out words.

The bottom half of a Bank of America cash machine receipt showing a balance of $21,452.35, interlined in neat, small cursive, in green ink from a fountain pen, continuing on the back.

A spiral notebook page, college-ruled, neatly folded twice, half-print/half-cursive hand in fine-point blue ballpoint in both Mandarin and English.

A strip of 8½ x 11 recycled printer paper, laser printed in 12-point Times New Roman font and cut from the page with scissors.

A yellow Post-It note pre-printed with a cat cartoon captioned "I refuse to engage in a battle of wits with an unarmed person," hand-printed in purple felt tip.

A torn square of white butcher paper, smelling of pastrami and sauerkraut, scrawled with brown chalk.

III. What Some of them Wished For

Casey Stone wished her parents, Molly and Tom, would stop arguing and like each other. Hector Hernandez wanted a 2015 Mustang GT convertible with an Oxford White exterior and the Reverse Sensing and Security Package, to replace his old Chevy Malibu beater that died a week ago, and a garage space to keep it safe, away from his block in East Palo Alto where it wouldn't last ten minutes.

Judy Liu asked for the biopsy of the lump she'd found in her right breast to come back negative. Sangeetha Sheshadri wished the blue plus on the Clearblue Easy stick was a false positive. Reginald Wentworth wished the blue plus on his wife's Clearblue Easy stick meant they'd have a girl after three boys.

Hannah McCarthy hoped for a smaller nose and bigger eyes and a way to attract Sanford. Jocelyn Peters wanted to lose 100 pounds of fat. Hartmut Denz wished to gain twenty pounds of muscle and to get shredded.

Grant Okeke wished his father would come home alive from his third tour in Afghanistan. Cody Spencer requested that Genentech buy his bio-tech startup before its second round of funding. Barney Oreglio prayed one of the six Megabucks tickets he purchased with the last of his disability check would hit big.

Sadie Levine longed for her mother to be alive to celebrate her becoming Bat Mitzvah. Gilbert Ali asked that his parents still love him once he came out to them. Misha Kotevsky just wanted someone in his family to get a living-wage job so he could stop eating at the St. Francis soup kitchen four times a week. Billy Sands wished for a new sleeping bag, a safe place to shower, and maybe even a place to live other than Burgess Park (unless that was too much to ask).

Marcella Santiago asked for three more wishes, and for those wishes to come true.

And because someone had to, Pierre Bischoff wished for immortality.

IV. Voices of Longing from the Wish-Fish Bowl

Lay-offs are next week and I'm a single mom, I can't lose this job. *I never asked nobody for nothing, not even God, but my baby girl, she come two months early and the doctors say her heart is all messed up.* Okay, I thought you heard me the first time but I guess not–or maybe you did and decided I'm not worthy for wishing for money enough to live like

Donald Trump for the rest of my life when kids are starving but who the fuck are you to judge me? *I don't mean to sound pushy, but how long does this usually take? I'm still waiting for Sanford to notice me.*

I tried to stop smoking, but I keep lighting up, even with the patch. Now they're telling me I got emphysema and I still can't stop smoking. *I wish for justice, for the people who did this to my beautiful daughter to be locked up for life. She never hurt anyone. She doesn't deserve what's happened to her.* I doubt you can help my Enrique, but maybe you can give me the strength to get through his illness to the end and be there for him when he leaves this life. *Please, just don't let me die before my kids are out of school, or at least before Sadie becomes Bat Mitzvah.*

I wish kids would stop bullying me online. Sometimes I feel like I can't take it anymore. I understand why those kids from Gunn and Paly lie down on the Caltrain tracks and end it all. *If I don't get an A in math this term, my father will disown me.* I'm so lonely. I just want someone to love me back for once. *Johan, I wish him to stop beating me.* I wish for world peace, because that's the kind of guy I am, as long as "peace" is broad enough to cover blow ups with judgmental, intolerant parents who voted for Prop 8. *I wish for an end to poverty and hunger. I'd be happy to start with my own.*

Grant my unborn baby health and safety. *It sounds stupid, but all I want is a good night's sleep. I haven't slept more than three hours at a stretch in years, and once I wake up, I'm up for hours. It's terrible.* I want my Yorkie puppy, Seymour, back. A car ran over him and he died. *I wish I saw a way out of this constant pain. The Caltrain tracks are looking really good right now.*

I wish it would rain. My plants are dying. If it doesn't rain soon, I'm going to have to rip out my yard and put in pebbles. *Can we please get this house? This is the fifth house we've bid on, way over the asking price, way more than we can afford, and every time we get screwed by some Valley millionaire who can plunk down hundreds of thousands of dollars above the asking price.*

I wish there was another Lucky Shanghai Dumpling truck and it was closer to my home in the East Bay. *I wish the Lucky Shanghai Dumpling truck would disappear and never come back. Look at all these people—they've become dependent on the idea of some magical, mystical, metaphysical solution to their problems. People come back, again and again. It's an addiction, a scourge. Worse than heroin.*

V. Which of the Wishes Would Have Been Granted, Had the Truck Not Disappeared?
We'll never know.

VI. Some of What Could Be Heard in the Parking Lot, Where the Truck Used to Park
"What will I do now?" *"What will we do now?"* Cries. *Wails.*
"What will happen to me now?" *"What will happen to my baby?"* "My child?" *"My husband?"* "My mother?" *Screams.* Keening.
"Will it come back?" *"Maybe it's around somewhere?"* "Maybe we can find it if we split up?" Nervous chatter. *Murmured compared notes.*
"Maybe all dumplings have this power. Has anyone tried wishing on dumplings from somewhere else?" *"Stop being a moron. You're not helping."* Ironic laughter. *Loud cursing, name calling.*
"This is somebody's fucking fault. Wait till I find out who." *"Maybe it's better this way. In the back of my mind, I always wondered whether the power might not be of the good."* Shouting. *Fists connecting with jawbones.* Prayers.
"We could, you know, involve the media. That consumer advocate on Channel 7."
"What about the police? FBI? Homeland Security? What about the company?"
"What will I do now?" *"What will we do now?"* Cries. *Wails.*
Silence.

VII. What the Company Had to Say
"Our records confirm that NoshTruck4You, Inc. never operated a food truck called 'Lucky Shanghai Dumpling' for its own account, nor have we ever leased a food truck to an entity operating under that name, or anything close to that name. We did have a truck go missing around the time the 'Lucky Shanghai Dumpling' truck allegedly first appeared. The company filed a police report, but the police never recovered that truck."
"We regret any inconvenience to our valued customers this confusion may have caused. Please enjoy our other fine mobile gourmet offerings. Download our app for locations and times."

VIII. No One Else Could Help
Captain Patricia O'Connor, Palo Alto Police Department, said that because the company had denied the truck's existence, no crime involving the Lucky Shanghai Dumpling truck (as opposed to the earlier-stolen truck) could have taken place. No

stolen property, no missing persons—once someone from the parking lot tracked down the two Nigerian college students who sold the dumplings, safe in their Stanford dorm room. Accordingly, the police had no jurisdiction over the matter.

Bloor Blomquist of Channel 7 said that, as the truck had not ripped off any consumers (on the contrary, it had many happy customers prior to its disappearance) *7 on Your Side* had no interest in pursuing the matter.

Homeland Security did not answer phone calls or emails.

Agent Bernard Embry of the FBI said that there was no evidence of a Federal crime. He was sorry, but the truck's disappearance did not amount to an act of terrorism.

Various members of the clergy reacted variously, depending upon their various interpretations of various scriptures and traditions. For some, the faith put in the dumplings amounted to blasphemy, and they counseled their flocks to renounce the dumplings. For others, the faith put in the dumplings actually demonstrated faith in God, or Jesus, or Allah, or one or more of many other gods, and they counseled their flocks to pray for strength to accept the change in their lives the truck's disappearance had wrought.

A couple of university professors promised to research the phenomenon, but said they could do nothing to change what had occurred. Though they might be able to explain it, eventually.

Late night talk show host Pepper Romeo, made some snide comments about those who believed in the dumplings' magic. She deleted her Twitter account in the wake of the shit storm that followed.

IX. Which of the Wishes Should Have Been Granted, Had the Truck Not Disappeared?

Most of the wishers, of course, thought their own wishes should have been granted. But if they had to pick one not their own, most of them would have voted for world peace or an end to poverty or hunger, which affected the planet generally and so also benefitted them.

Three generous wishers would have voted to grant the wishes they deemed most desperate and necessary, but none were willing to reveal their votes.

X. The Languor of Despair, the Resurgence of Optimism

Some of the wishers, concerned about privacy, retrieved their wishes from the fishbowl and destroyed them. Some kept them, pressed into a book like a dried flower, or in a nightstand drawer like a lock of hair, and took them out wistfully from time to time as they would a flower or lock of hair.

Some left the wishes in the bowl, just in case. Some never came back while the wishing bowl still stood in the parking lot, and only learned much later what had happened. By then it was too late to take back the wishes, even if the wishers had been so inclined.

After a few weeks, a new food truck started occupying the space the Lucky Shanghai Dumpling truck once frequented, but only on Mondays and Wednesdays. This truck, The Whole Shebang, sold hamburgers. This truck also kept a fishbowl for business card raffles on its counter. A few former Lucky Shanghai Dumpling customers tried wishing on cheeseburgers, with bacon and avocado.

If any of those wishes came true, no one talked about it. The Whole Shebang did a brisk business, but no lines ever snaked through the parking lot, down the sidewalk, and into the oak grove.

Some wishers wished on other dumplings at other food trucks and restaurants, but no reports surfaced of these wishes coming true.

It was said:

The Lucky Shanghai Dumpling truck would come back when people proved worthy in their wishes. The Lucky Shanghai Dumpling truck would never come back, because the majority of wishers were too selfish, something that would never change as long as humans were humans.

The Lucky Shanghai Dumpling truck never left. It was straddling two parallel universes, the fishbowl and the Nigerian college students in this universe, the rest of the truck in the other. The Lucky Shanghai Dumpling truck would come back tomorrow, or when the drama died down, or when everyone least expected it.

The Lucky Shanghai Dumpling truck would never come back because it had never actually been there in the first place. Some mass hallucination had caused thousands of people to believe they had made a wish, eaten dumplings and, in some cases, had their wishes granted. The granted wishes, too, were a massive delusion, caused by chemical spills, cosmic radiation, or perhaps something in the water supply. After all, the entire area suffered from severe drought. Couldn't that affect the water supply?

The dumplings helped a lot of people. But now those people would have to help each other and themselves, just as they had before the truck arrived. The dumplings made people feel hopeful, and now people would have to find hope somewhere else.

It was also said:

The dumplings had been a blessing. The dumplings had been a curse.

The dumplings had no effect whatsoever. Whatever they seemed to do would have happened anyway. They merely emboldened the wishers to make positive changes in their own lives. They merely led the wishers to other like-minded people whose positive energy merged with their own to affect outcomes.

Eventually, life returned to normal. In a few years, the food truck craze died a natural death, and food trucks no longer congregated in the parking lot behind the defunct train station.

The Lucky Shanghai Dumpling truck became the stuff of suburban legend, along with the secret night time activities of NASA at the Stanford Dish, the radio telescope atop a hill overlooking Interstate 280.

But those who swore the dumplings granted their wishes believed until their lives ended that without the dumplings, they would never again have a chance at obtaining the greatest desires of their hearts.

Or, that having once been gifted with an inexplicable manifestation of the greatest desires of their hearts, there was every reason to expect something just as wonderful would happen again.

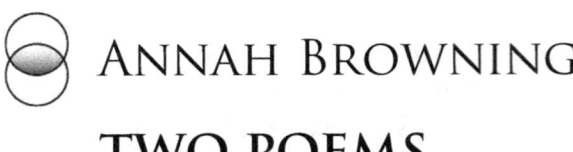

Annah Browning

TWO POEMS

THE HOUSE SAYS I LOVE YOU

Thin slivers of you
embed in me, like glass

in wood—your hair and your
nails. What you wind and

what you cut. I am struck
through with silver

lights, and you wander
like a song, trailing

your chorus. One after
another, your voices go

slack in your throats
like isolated flowers, dark

down to their beginnings.
Sediment is a form

of love—to take on layers,
to compress soot dust

and spider to this fineness—
a grain that marks, that

marks all trespassers—
I feel you, your fingernails

in the wallpaper, curling
it back, evergreen

to black mold sprinkling
silent as the surface

of the moon. Lean into me,
turn a finger-length key—now

revolve, revolve. I won't
give you up.

WITCH AS LA BELLE DAME

Don't forget to love me.
I require it, my milky eyes
require it, and furthermore

I won't let you get farther
than the sycamore tree.
Lie down and be a map

for dew and frost, my finger-
nail traced paths, for
the changelings I will

beget and leave forgot.
Turn your head a little.
Tilt, planetary—this ear

gets a vernal equinox,
sun-crossed, and every
rabbit I send for you

to eat will only be
a little rabid, a little
lean—oh isn't this

the privacy you wanted?
This night is the good
bath. I'm going to lick you
clean— sans merci—

ALAN M. CLARK

Study for The Sticks

# C. Samuel Rees

ARSENIKESSER

She and her name weren't on speaking terms
each digit was a phial three measures venomous
blooming bliss   then itch   then melt with touch
      holds her own hand in bed
sleeps almond-scented   withers night
      convalesces but never cures

Brimming she tracks distant orbits
      pairs   trios   orgies
      the joyful solipsist   a wreck of lovers
she paints each toe a coral snake
colors herself dangerous
      eyelids heavy water   low-level immunity
      in bed no one does any saving

Each day a revenant's lesson
      kudzu   hemlock   nightshade
this bella donna of decline
when she infects the room scent slips on a protective hood
      hypodermic intrusion
snapped stems   blasted buds   muddled tonics
      every bone-corseted alley   enraptured hallway
narrow-minded vestibule abandons itself to her

Insomniac-steeped she sits long nights in the county morgue
      extends each drawer like a beckoning

reclines each finger on impermanent lips
       sips silence to dilute her discontent
      this error
            her everything

 ROBERT GUFFEY

THE SHEET

1. Carter leaped out of bed,
grabbed his perspiration-stained sheet, and dashed into the hall fully naked. Gray, diffuse sunlight filled the hallway. It was probably about six o'clock in the morning. Everybody in the building would be waking soon.

He swung open the bathroom door and proceeded to stuff the sheet down the toilet. It was his favorite with which to cover up. He liked the way it felt, the way it looked: beige, the color of faded memory, or cream in coffee. The word "sleep" could be seen on every inch of the cotton fabric, microscopically, almost subliminally.

Somehow, by pushing the fabric downward inch by inch, and with repeated flushings, he was able to expunge almost half the sheet before the rumbling began.

2. The entire apartment began to slide—
no, not slide, but *roll*. Yes, it rolled right out into the middle of the street. From his living room window (he was on the second floor) he could see a horde of cars swerving to avoid a collision with the mobile building.

He could see so clearly at that moment: the expressions of fear and surprise on the faces of the drivers down below as they attempted to swerve their vehicles out of the way. One driver stood out: a long-haired gentleman wearing sunglasses and stylish clothes with a cell phone pressed to his ear. He seemed like the type of person in desperate need of a good scare.

Sudden life-threatening accidents can have profound effects on the right personality types, thought Carter. Perhaps this is why the universe goes a little crazy sometimes—for the benefit of the inmates. He thought of his favorite Fortean quote: "If there is a universal mind, must it be sane?"

Carter was very pleased with himself, despite the fact that he'd had very little to do with the building having gone berserk. He hadn't *intended* on this result. He hadn't intended on any results at all. He'd simply felt the urge to stuff his sheet down the toilet, that's all.

3. The building didn't kill anyone,

not outright. It destroyed a lot of private property, of course. He saw white picket fences and gingerbread houses and cats and dogs and entertainment systems tossed aside like wet cardboard under the brunt of the on-rushing domicile. The true danger arose when they hit the freeway. He didn't know how they managed to maneuver through the tight curves of the on-ramp, but maneuver through them they did. Judging from the landmarks whizzing by, he soon ascertained that they were heading north on the 405 in the general direction of Santa Monica. Toward the sea.

It was early on a Saturday morning and the traffic was sparse. Most of the cars were able to pull off to the side, to safety, long before the building was anywhere near them. However, Carter soon became aware of the sound of rotary blades close overhead and sirens on his tail. He sat down in front of the TV and flipped through the channels until he hit a local news station. To his surprise, he was treated to a bird's-eye-view of his own apartment building as it raced down the 405 pursued by a flotilla of L.A.'s finest. The anchor, a distinguished-looking gray-haired gentleman named Abe Fischman, told the audience that this was the strangest police pursuit he'd seen in all his years of broadcasting. His co-anchor, an attractive young Latina, began thinking out loud, questioning the validity of airing such escapist fare. Fischman turned on her and sniped, "What're you talking about? This is in the interest of public safety!" "Public safety?" the woman said, laughing. "The only people in danger are on the freeway. You think they're watching TV?" Before Fischman could reply, the scene cut away to a close-up shot of Carter's own rooftop. He saw an old man standing on the edge. The old man flung his metal walker aside, then held his arms out like an orchestra conductor, like a man about to fly.

"Oh, shit," Carter muttered beneath his breath. It was Grossinger from #8. A sweet old fellow, a veteran of the Vietnam War. Carter had often brought him food from the deli he worked at part-time. The two of them would sit around, drink beer (though Grossinger's doctor insisted he shouldn't have any alcohol), and listen to the old radio shows Carter recorded off KNX sometimes. Grossinger's favorite was *X-Minus One*. Carter liked *The Shadow*. Grossinger actually remembered hearing some of them when they were first broadcast. Sometimes Carter wished he could go back to that era. It seemed innocent somehow, untainted.

Grossinger often talked about going back to those times too, though usually in the context of death. He was suicidal, had been since the passing of his wife three years before.

From what the cameras were showing Carter, he'd decided at long last to join her on the Other Side.

4. Carter shot up from his chair,

slipped on a pair of tattered Levis and flip-flop sandals, and burst out the front door, hoping he wasn't already too late to save his friend. He passed two of his neighbors on the open-air deck outside—the obese couple in #3, the freakazoids who liked to play their porno flicks far too loud for Carter's taste. They wanted to stop and discuss the hows and whys of the building's abrupt mobility, but Carter just waved them away and told them, "Another time." Couldn't they see he had more important things to do?

The only way up onto the roof was the handyman's ladder. Grossinger must have pulled it out of the storage room, for it still stood against the edge of the roof right in front of the door to Apt. #6. Mr. and Mrs. Arbuckle (who knew their real names?) stared at Carter, sloe-eyed and confused, as he scuttled up the rickety wooden steps with the speed of a panicked monkey. The roof was covered with gravel that crunched beneath his sandals as he ran toward Grossinger. The poor old man's arms were held out in a cruciform, and the blades of a distant police copter seemed—for an instant—like a halo surrounding his seventy-seven-year-old head.

"Please, God, my Lord and Saviour, take me back to Martha!" Grossinger yelled as his whole body tensed.

"Don't do it!" Carter screamed, knowing he could not reach the man in time.

"If you say so," Grossinger said, stepping down from the ledge. He breathed a sigh of relief. "Man, I thought you'd never come."

Carter bent over at the waist, resting his hands on his knees, and tried to catch his breath. "You mean you never meant to—?"

"No," Grossinger said, lowering himself to the rooftop. "No one wants me anymore. I'm a burden to everyone... most importantly, myself. I don't know what's going to happen, I just know I ruined everything. I thought I might have a chance to live a full life, but now I don't know."

"Oh, c'mon. You've lived a full life."

Grossinger rose to his feet once more. "I know there is something else out there way more important than this fucked-up country on a fucked planet and I will find it because that is where I belong. Not here!" Suddenly, he attempted to fling himself over the roof.

Carter grabbed Grossinger's right wrist and shirttail at the last second and reeled him back in. The old man tried to wriggle out of Carter's grasp, but Carter managed to wrestle him to the ground. An uncomfortable moment of silence followed as they sat there amidst the gravel, Carter's arm draped across the old man's shoulders. "I... what should I do now?" Carter asked.

"Convince me I have a lot to live for."

Carter tried to think of something. He pulled at his lower lip, as he often did when thinking intently. "When's the last time you went to the beach?"

Grossinger's eyes rolled upward. "Oh, so long ago I can't even remember."

"Then it's about time you saw it again. And judging by the speed we're going I'd say we'll be there in about... thirty minutes."

"Martha always liked the beach," Grossinger said, staring off into space. "She was from Iowa. She couldn't believe there could be that much water in the whole world."

The loss and sadness in his voice were so tangible, Carter could almost picture the two of them, Grossinger and his wife, sitting on the beach and watching the waves roll in. Carter realized he didn't even know what Martha looked like. Grossinger had no photographs of her.

At that moment Carter noticed the police helicopter lowering ever closer to the rooftop. The pilot was waving at them, shouting reassurances. The cop on the passenger side began to lower a ladder down to them.

"No!" Grossinger said, clutching the front of Carter's shirt. "I don't want to go. I-I want to see the beach. I want to see the ocean. One last time at least."

Carter patted him on the shoulder. "You don't have to do anything you don't want to do." The rope ladder hit the gravel only a few feet away from them. They turned their backs on it, heading instead toward the wooden ladder that would lead them to their respective homes.

When they reached the deck below, the Arbuckle family was still standing there, staring at the two men with their dull, dead eyes.

"Wh-what's it like up there?" the woman asked, her pink fingernails digging into the back of her husband's pudgy hand. Her husband stared at the pair with equal intensity.

"It's just a roof," Carter said. "Why don't you go up there and see for yourselves?"

"Oh, we could never do that," the husband said. "We're not in good enough shape to make the climb. Besides, what if we never got down again?"

Carter shrugged. "Doesn't matter to me if you see it or not. It's your choice."

5. He pushed past them

and led the old man into Carter's apartment. Before he shut the door Carter took one last look at the Arbuckles. They remained on the deck, staring up at the roof with longing in their eyes, as if waiting for angels to descend from the heavens and lift them up. They'd be waiting a long time.

Upon entering his living room, Carter was met with simultaneous cries from his twelve roommates. They were always most demanding at breakfast time.

"I see all the commotion finally woke you guys up," Carter said.

Grossinger bent down and scratched Trombly behind the ears. "I thought they were supposed to warn us about events like this," Grossinger said.

"Not my cats," Carter said as he filled twelve different bowls with twelve different combinations of organic grains made specifically for felines. Each of them preferred a different brand. "Mine just lie around and get fat."

"Sort of like me."

"Don't feel bad. The Egyptians emulated cats, why not you?" With the sound of the grains shuffling around in the box, Carter's roommates came running. Carter had to raise his voice in order to hear himself over the purring. "So what do you say? We've got about thirty minutes before we hit the beach. How about an old radio show?"

Grossinger settled down into the sofa next to the lamp, his favorite spot. He formed his fingers into a steeple and rested them against his upper lip. "What would do the trick right about now? *Suspense*? 'My Son John'?"

"Too intense."

"Point taken. *Chandu the Magician*? The first chapter of *Return of Roxxor*?"

"Not intense enough."

"Yeah, I guess. Ah, I have it! *Adventures by Morse*. 'Dead Men Prowl.'"

"Now you're talkin' hamburger language." Carter finished feeding his roommates, then strolled over to his "entertainment system"—a Sony Radio Cassette-Corder CFM-104 encased within the hollow shell of an old-time radio, the proper kind of radio, the one built in the shape of a Greco-Roman archway.

Grossinger looked confused. "What'd you just say?"

"Hamburger language! You know, it's like what Captain Beefheart once said: 'There are forty people in the world, and five of them are hamburgers.' That's what you and me are, Grossinger. We're hamburgers."

"Is that good or bad?"

"Neither." Carter swung the casing aside, then popped in his copy of 'Dead Men Prowl' Chapter 1.

First the sound of a clock tower striking twice. Next the baritone announcer breaks in: "*Adventures by Morse!*" Then the high-pitched wailing of what sound like air raid sirens as the announcer continues: "Carlton E. Morse presents... 'Dead Men Prowl' featuring Captain Friday!" The actor portraying Captain Friday intones, "If you like high adventure... come with me. If you like blood and thunder—" A massive thunderclap rips through the airwaves. "Come with me."

They listened all the way to the end of Chapter 1, when Captain Friday sees the corpse of old Doc Simms shambling along the fog-shrouded beach, then leaped out of their chairs in fright when a scream burst in upon them from outside.

"What the hell was that?" Grossinger said.

"Sounds like that fat couple from #3." Carter pulled the curtain aside and saw Mrs. Arbuckle still standing on the porch, pointing downward. At the Pacific Ocean.

The building was sinking into the sea. They must have been travelling faster than Carter had calculated.

"Looks like you're about to get your wish!" Carter called back to the old man.

"We made it to the beach?"

"No, I meant your *first* wish... the one about dying."

"But I was just joshing!"

"Too bad, man. I guess God doesn't have much of a sense of humor—anymore."

Grossinger rose from the sofa and limped over to Carter. "Can't we climb back onto the roof?"

"What's the point? It'll just delay the inevitable." The water was over the deck now. Both the Arbuckles began screeching in terror. They ran toward the ladder at the same time, fighting over who would climb up first. Mr. Arbuckle beat his wife in the face, leaving her flat on her back, then grabbed hold of the rungs. He shot up that ladder faster than Carter ever would have thought possible. Unfortunately, the Pacific had coated the entire deck, causing it to be slippery. The second Arbuckle reached the final rung the ladder slid backwards, toppling over like a felled redwood. It crashed against the top of the deck railing and sent Arbuckle splashing down into the ocean. It didn't look like he could swim very well. He sank like a thirteen ton rock. His wife wasted no time. She righted the ladder and tried to climb up herself—to the same disastrous end.

Carter just shook his head and closed the door. "Won't be long now. You want to hear the beginning of Chapter 2?"

Grossinger clung to Carter's shirt collar. "Why is this happening, *why*?"

"I'm sorry, I think it's my fault. It's because of the dream."

Grossinger let go of Carter's shirt. "What do you mean? What dream?"

Carter shrugged. "I don't remember. It had something to do with spider webs."

Grossinger glanced over at the television set, which was still playing the news. There they were: an aerial shot of the building, sinking fast. Then: a full shot of all the beach bums and truant school kids, watching in fascination as the building sank. Many of the kids were laughing.

Grossinger pointed the remote at the TV, flipped the station to 00. Carter couldn't figure out what he was doing... until he saw it. Right in front of him, all over again. How on earth could...?

"So is that it?" Grossinger said, pointing at the screen. "Is that what you dreamed?"

Carter didn't say anything. He didn't have to. His dream was already in progress, preserved there inside that box exactly as he had experienced it a little over an hour before. It all came back to him as the dream unfolded before his eyes once more, some of it in full color, most of it in black and white.

Carter was trapped in a silk cocoon, suspended in space above a white marble staircase that spiraled down into darkness. There were people at the bottom of the staircase. A lot of them. Carter couldn't see them, but he knew they were there. He could hear them, hear them laughing at him.

The spiders. They were all over him. Only his face was visible through the cocoon. He looked pale, too pale, as if the blood had been drained out of him. He screamed. The spiders swarmed up his body, toward his eyes and ears and open mouth.

Carter touched his fingers to the TV screen in a fruitless attempt to brush the creepy-crawlies away. He was surprised when his hand went right through the glass, as if the screen itself were made of silk. The spiders burst out of the TV and covered his arm within seconds. Their legs felt like invasive needle pricks.

He called out to Grossinger for help.

The old man backed away toward the front door, shaking his head. "I-I'm going back up on the roof. I've still got time. This is all your fault, it's always been your fault."

"No, no, don't—!"

Too late. Grossinger swung the door open; the ocean came pouring in. Carter had no choice, no choice at all. He'd drown if he didn't. He crawled through the TV screen, back into the dream.

6. He closed his eyes and mouth

as the arachnids covered every inch of his body. He shook from side to side, growing more enraged than frightened, and breathed a sigh of relief as he heard the thin strands snap and his cocoon drop through the cool black air. Something inside him cracked when he hit the staircase. His body tumbled down the massive stairs and landed with a thud on a sandy beach. The spiders abandoned him upon impact and scattered, crawling up the sequin dresses worn by the beautiful Victorian ladies who surrounded him. The ladies didn't scream. Quite the contrary. They smiled and danced with one another while Rachmaninov's "The Isle of the Dead" played in the background from some unknown source.

Carter ripped out of his cocoon as the ladies did the same. They removed their dresses, revealing bodies that had been stripped of flesh, leaving only raw musculature exposed. The spiders danced along their hourglass curves, fashioning new skin from silk. The ladies moaned, as if in glorious ecstasy.

Carter crawled away from them, toward the ocean, his broken legs trailing behind him like someone else's bones. Not until he was already submerged in this sea did he realize how much warm blood tainted its purity. How many people had recently died here? He glanced behind him and saw the ladies strolling up the staircase, hand-in-hand, toward a gray sky filled with cobwebs. The ocean embraced him. He swam, tried to at least, but his broken legs dragged him down. The deeper Carter went, the more the water felt like webs tightening about his face.

7. Too late. Grossinger

swung the door open; the ocean came pouring in. Carter had no choice, no choice at all.

He'd drown if he didn't. He began to crawl through the TV screen, back into the dream.

No. He stopped himself. Wait, he thought, wait... you always have a choice....

Even with his arm stuck inside the TV screen all the way up to his elbow, Carter managed to stop his descent. He glanced to his right and saw the old-fashioned, Greco-Roman radio sitting on the nightstand. Of course....

He managed to pluck his arm out of the silky stickiness of the glass screen as the Pacific poured into the living room up to his waist. He trudged through the icy cold water, thrust his left arm into the left speaker of the radio.

He penetrated the past, emerged like a cabbage patch fetus from the sand of a cool white beach on an island just off the coast of... where? The distant, winking lights of San Francisco couldn't have been more distinctive. It was night and he was surrounded by mist. A woman screamed somewhere in the darkness. A young woman? No doubt. An incandescent skeleton wrapped in a flowing black robe darted past him in the gibbous moonlight. Oh, the night was filled with wondrous and frightening mysteries. It was time someone began solving them. Carter pushed himself all the way out of the soft sand and chased after the gibbering skeleton-man, ordering the dead thing to halt, knowing (unlike poor old Grossinger) that he had Death on the run at long last.

 VIRGINIA SHREVE

TWO POEMS

PEAR, COYOTE, MOON

Half-past the sturgeon moon
coyote sends his shadow
slipping like slubbed silk
through the stubbled meadow

Heavy-headed asters bob
along the border of the yard
hunchbacked pear tree sighs
the stem too tight the flesh
in bloom you must wait

wait another moon

Harvest moon or Hunter
muzzles dipped
in the rotting fruit, shoulders grind
in the slime of fermented pears
Drunken coyotes
dance and bite
howl wild the rampage canis bacchanal
yips like the points of stars
broken off and shattered like glass
upon the astonished grass
yellow eyes gleam
like tiny renegade moons
no thought but body

the body a god the moon a god the pears
small perfect Buddhas of inebriate gods

There should perhaps be poodles
behind the window of the house.

They fall silent in the face of such display
Grateful no doubt for warm bed food always
in the bowl, but does one wish for just one moment
to wear a black leather jacket
the teeth of small mammals like a necklace
and ride
with the coyotes?

Next day it is like the aftermath of any fraternity kegger
Stench, and piles of puke, and memories left crawling
away from the sun

A LITTLE HELP FROM MY FRIENDS

I shall choose as an appropriate setting
for my demise
an improbable Rousseau jungle
populated
by large-billed birds in green
and scarlet guise,
speckled panthers,
leering baboons;
bordering a smooth white shore
a coral-toothed blue
lagoon
About noon a low-down and
dusky
jazz trombonist
comes strolling down the beach
he wears white shoes
and white white teeth
sun glints off that long-necked horn –
"Take five," he says,
waltzing by
(Probably I'll wear a rubber nose and
paint my face for the occasion)
Beardsley and Sappho will be there
sitting on a washed-up palm
They are slumming, but
politely attentive
Beardsley, elegantly
consumptive
has bony wrists
has forgotten his ink pot.
Sappho, lush as the foliage,
red red lips

black hair oiled
coiled around her head,
petals linger on her skirts –
tells me the dawn has gold sandals
 why don't I make it another day –
Around twilight
Aubrey and S. start a round
of "Who's on first?"
I decide it's time,
take off my watch
pay the balloon seller,

(the pier is long long and narrow
I believe there is a diving board at the end
where my brother waves)
And take my final bow.

Many small fish applaud

 LYNN PATTISON

TWO POEMS

NEAR STREAMS I SOMETIMES THINK I HEAR HER

I don't know when water first started becoming her. We noticed footprints in the hall when it hadn't rained, puddles on the linoleum. Thinking back, her voice seemed to bubble, somehow, up from her throat, her gaze had grown watery. Her knees got runny and we'd catch her just as she was going down. When she sat on the sofa all her parts seemed to seek the same level. Soon we had to carry her to church in the wheelbarrow, careful not to slosh. We kept the kids at a distance. At night she reflected the moon, illuminating the porch. I thought I saw her skin ripple in the breeze. For a while she wanted bowls around her—on the floor, the bed, her chair and took to sleeping in the tub. In the end she only wanted to go to the river—we could only refuse so many times. When the day came, we all went together to the swimming hole but we knew she wasn't coming home again. When she eased in the current, we said our goodbyes and mumbled our prayers. We know she is always with us, in the rain, the snow, the summer lake.

I PLANTED IT UNDER A GIANT CYPRESS

She put her womb in our old valise. Brown leather, buckles and straps. Shoved it in a corner of the pump house, said she didn't need that worry when there was all the rest. I knew it wasn't the worry but the weight, how it grew heavier each year, filling with portend, regret. At times it hummed, a droning flute. When she wanted to throw it down the well, I took it away. Seven miles and into the bog, past the school, past the cemetery. Told no one. She never asked after it. I don't know exactly when women started visiting—tying ribbons, setting little dolls or scrolls of words among the roots. They sing. Those who come alone may bring a small bag. They leave empty-handed. No music then.

 CHRIS KAMMERUD

MAEMI

Miyoko follows a trail of feathers and blood over mountains and seas, across time and forests, through sunlight and shade. She is searching for her heart. A bird stole it.

Fucking birds.

In her right hand, Miyoko carries a white card with her name written on it. It's not really her name, but it's the one she's holding onto at the moment. On her back, there is a violin which sometimes she plays to earn her way. Moving on has its costs. Miyoko has learned before how to be still, and she can't take it anymore. At the ocean, where the trail of feathers and blood ends, she climbs up to the sun and asks, "Have you seen a magpie fly this way? One as dark as the burnt rocks of Hallasam? One around whose neck hangs a chestnut?"

The sun says, "Mollahyo," which means I don't know. "Perhaps, yes. Maybe a long time ago. Maybe yesterday. I am so old sometimes I forget how time works. I'm sorry I can't be more specific. But, here's a very small and magical casket which you may open when things seem hopeless, as they so often do."

"Ssibal," Miyoko says, which means you've got to be fucking kidding me.

"Also, there's a boat over there," the sun says. "You could probably take that across the sea if you want. I believe that is where the magpie flew whenever it was that it flew this way."

Miyoko takes the casket with a frown. She remembers the sun being different before. But maybe it was just that she was a girl then, and now she is older and less infatuated with whimsy.

Miyoko gets on the boat. She shows the captain her card. He nods. The captain wears a faded, wool sweatshirt and tattered jeans. He is a smooth and wiry old man, eroded by wind and water. His name is Nam-gi. He asks her if she'd like him to store her violin and very small casket below deck. She says no. She says she doesn't trust that things will return to her if she lets them go.

He says, "What is it the Americans say? If you love something, set it free?"

Miyoko says, "Ssibal," and retires.

The boat sets sail. Miyoko lies in bed, afraid to close her eyes, the casket and violin held tight to either side. She listens to the ocean beat against the walls of her cabin. It sounds like footsteps. She can't sleep.

Once upon a time there was a world, a war, and a girl. The girl lived with her two older sisters and their father in Samcheok-eup, a village on the eastern coast of Korea between the Taebaek mountains and the East Sea. They were poor, but so was everyone else in their village, especially once the Japanese arrived. Around her home grew chestnut, white pine, and persimmon trees. The sun spoke to her of summer. The moon of autumn. In the spring, the girl ran through rolling fields of garlic, pepper, and chrysanthemum, chasing grasshoppers and listening to the locusts, their constant song, rising and falling, with each shushing step, with each beat of her heart. Maemi, they said. Maemi. A song of waking, after years trapped underground.

Her father worked in the mountains, digging gold from the mines in the nearby caves of Jeongseon. He explained once to his daughters about amalgamation, mixing fistfuls of rock and mercury in a pan. Placed over a fire, the mixture bubbled until the mercury melted away taking everything with it but the gold, shining happily in your pan.

"Like a fairy tale," the eldest daughter said.

"Time and fire," the middle daughter said.

"And then happily ever after," said the girl, their little, bright-eyed sister.

The daughters dug garlic from the fields and hung them on racks to dry. They harvested rice. Japanese gendarmes gathered all of the gold and most of the crop for themselves, of course, as tax, as payment for the family's debt to the empire. No one was sure where the debt came from, but the Japanese assured them that they owed their lives to the emperor and so everything belonged to him. In the evenings, the father returned home from the mines, with chapped lips and scaled hands, and was always greeted first by his youngest daughter because she loved him most of all--also because she had less chores to do being so young. After dinner, he tucked his girls into mats warmed by the steaming ondol, his kisses imprinting on their foreheads the smell of dirt and the fading promise of fortune.

One day, the girl's father said he was going to Seoul to buy them each a gift for their hard work.

The girl asked her father where he got the money.

Her father put a finger over his lips and patted his heavy pocket.

The eldest daughter asked for the sly, soft fur of a fox.

The middle daughter said she wanted a small, jade pendant carved into the shape of the crescent moon.

The youngest daughter said she wanted only three good, strong pieces of string so that she could build a violin out of wood from an old rice chest.

The father promised to bring back what he could.

In Seoul, he found the strings quite easily. The jade, as well, though it cost him everything he had. He scoured Namdaemun for hours and couldn't find the sly, soft fur of a fox. He was heartbroken. He did not want to face his daughters having fulfilled for them only a portion of his promise. He began his journey back, though, prepared for failure, hoping to find the words to express how some promises couldn't be kept. But, outside of a small town in Ganwon-do, at the edge of a forest, resting atop the stump of a chopped elm, there was a fox, glistening red and dark and dead. The father walked over and picked it up, amazed at his luck.

Before he could place the fur in his bag, he heard the cocking of a pistol aimed, presumably, somewhere in the vicinity of his chest.

"I can't let you take that," a voice said.

The father turned. A kempei, a Japanese policeman with the imperial chrysanthemum stitched on his jacket's lapel, leaned against a cherry tree.

"It's just a fox," the father said. "It belongs to the land. To whoever finds it."

"It belongs to whoever tracked and shot the bitch."

"Please," the father said. "It's for my daughter."

The kempei said, "How many children do you have?"

The father said, "I have no sons to donate to the glorious effort of Japan, only three daughters."

"Only daughters?"

"Yes."

"I could let you take the bitch fur," the kempei said, "but I would have to follow you home, and, whomever of your house greeted you first, I would take as payment for the fur and any outstanding debts you may have."

"My daughters are not for sale," the father said, thinking of his youngest and the way her eyes blinked when overwhelmed with excitement.

"It's a good deal. One girl and your family is free."

The father thought of this, and felt lighter, and then sick. "I couldn't," he said.

"What is it the Americans say? If you love something, set it free?"

"Mollahyo."

"Besides it could be a chicken, or dog, that greets me first. Do you have chickens? A dog?"

"Yes."

"Perhaps fate will smile on you."

The father let himself imagine keeping all of the gold from the mountain and all of the garlic from their land. He let himself imagine sending his daughters to school, to something, to somewhere. He let himself imagine there was such a thing as luck.

When he returned home, his youngest daughter met him first, of course. Luck didn't exist. Not for him. His youngest daughter hugged him, overcome with joy at the sight of the three strong strings looped around his belt. Her eyes blinked and blinked and then stopped.

"Who's that man?" she said, looking over her father's shoulder.

Her father put her and his sack down.

The girl's two sisters came and pulled their gifts from the bag. The eldest wrapped the fur around her shoulders. The middle child held the crescent jade up to her eyes.

The father saw how beautiful and happy his older daughters were, and he began to cry, understanding the cost of their joy. He pulled his bright-eyed, youngest daughter close and whispered in her ear, "Run!"

The kempei struck her father's temple with the butt of his pistol. He grabbed the girl's wrist before she had taken a single step. "A promise is a promise," the kempei said. He led the girl away.

Miyoko steps quietly across the deck, her eyes searching the night-bright sky for a bird that stole her heart. She hears the crew. She joins them in the captain's cabin. She drinks sake and plays a Japanese card game, Battle of the Flowers. The captain has a knife-thin scar across his cheek. His mate smokes a cigarette. The men ask Miyoko where she came from, and where she is going.

In Battle of the Flowers, the cards are divided into twelve suits, each suit corresponding to a month and flower. March, for example, being cherry blossoms. Within each suit, there are four cards, whose point values are unnecessary and, for the most part, completely arbitrary. The goal of the game is not so much to collect points, as it is to gather certain combinations, or amalgamations, of time and foliage.

Miyoko says, "I'm from Samcheok-eup, by way of somewhere faraway, and now I'm on my way home."

"You're Korean?" the first mate says.

"Yes."

"But your name," the captain says.

"Is my business."

The first mate says, "What's the casket for?"

The captain kicks his first mate's foot.

"What?" the first mate says.

Miyoko says, "Mollahyo." She collects combinations of cherry blossoms and Novembers and pulls the amalgamations close to her. "It seems to be part of a pattern of late wherein the universe delivers a lot of nonsense into my life."

"Hey," the mate says, "don't twist the cards like that."

"Sorry," says Miyoko.

The captain grumbles. He turns over another card. Miyoko wins again. The ocean rolls along under the ship. Miyoko's small stack of amalgamations and contradictions falls onto the floor. The captain chews on the tip of his tongue. He decides to speak. He says, "You have a lot of luck for such a small girl."

"I've never had any luck," the first mate says, drawing cards. "When I was born, I came out backwards and blue."

Miyoko says, "You wouldn't say that about me having luck if you knew my story."

"What's your story?" says the captain.

"A lot of nonsense," says Miyoko.

"Is it scary?" the first mate says.

"Listen," says Miyoko.

The men lean close. The ocean beats against the ship. Miyoko pauses, afraid, but then begins.

"Once upon a time," she says.

The girl's father gave her a yellow cardigan that once belonged to her mother. She wore it on the cold morning a truck drove her to the sea, where she took that first boat to Japan. The kempei who took her was named Aki. He chided the girl for crying at the vanishing horizon of her home. "You'll forget it soon enough," he said. "Time is your friend. It will take away everything you no longer need."

The girl was with other girls who were going to other places. Some of them to Tokyo or Shimonoseki, to work in airplane or munition factories. Some to Manchuria or Nanking to work on the front-lines, washing clothes and providing comfort for the Japanese soldiers.

The girl went to southeastern China, to serve in an ianjo, a comfort station or recreation camp, a place where the men, tired from war, could relax and take pleasure. The station was constructed into something like a house, consisting of a single hallway with several small, adjoining rooms to either side. It was part of a Japanese military camp. Aki told her that there were three orders she must follow as a member of the Volunteer Labor Corps of Japan.

She was to stay in her room until told to leave.

She was never to speak unless spoken to.

She was to follow any other orders which she received from any other Japanese soldier.

"If you follow these three orders," Aki said, "you will return home to your family as a hero."

They stood inside a narrow wooden room on whose door hung a sign etched with the girl's new name, Miyoko. The room had a small cot and chamber pot. The cot had a single sheet and no pillow. In the pot, she was meant to wash her clothes and the soldiers' condoms. A small window opposite her looked out at a tiny mosaic of sky, veined by branches of an old chestnut tree.

Aki ordered the girl to remove her clothes.

They stood in the room. The girl had never been so close to a man before. She was afraid. He leaned towards her as though she possessed some gravity over him. Cicadas buzzed outside the window. Maemi, they said. Maemi. The girl whispered to them to stay underground.

"What was that?" Aki said.

"Nothing," the girl said.

Sweat fell down her spine and pooled in the hollows of her knees. She had never taken her clothes off in front of anyone that she could remember other than her sisters.

Aki asked her if she heard him.

She nodded.

The girl serviced dozens of soldiers per day. After sunset, only officers, like Aki, were allowed. There were so many, some wanting a full hour, some leaving after five minutes. Some still dusted with sun and blood, some smelling of gunpowder and ginger. Once they discovered her talent with rhythm, they asked her to sing. They gave her a violin when she asked. They said it had belonged to someone else. Someone who didn't need it now. Their bodies blurred, their faces vanished. She named them after trees and flowers. She sang songs about them. They didn't understand. She didn't understand them either. The songs or the men. Here was the pine tree, full of rough bark and sharp needles, that wanted and wanted. Here was the plum blossom, bruised and squat, that begged and begged. Here was the willow, soft and slender, that wept and wept.

A forest grew inside the girl's heart.

The girl ate rice and chestnuts for breakfast, lunch, and dinner. Sometimes in the early evening, she sat in the hallway of the ianjo among the other girls, all, like her, with names scratched into boards of wood that hung on the doors behind them. Officers and important visitors were allowed to choose.

One night, after a sad, but violent, cherry blossom tree twisted her into pieces, she put herself back together and looked in the liquid mirror of the chamber pot and spoke her new name Miyoko, again and again, forming her lips around the strange sounds until the strangeness melted away. She cracked open a chestnut she'd saved from dinner. She replaced the nut with the heart of a girl who ran with grasshoppers and hummed with locusts. She closed the shell with a kiss and buried it beneath her bed.

Midnight on the sea, in her cabin, trying to fall asleep again in the boat the sun told her to take across the sea, Miyoko hears the door open. She feels a weight on the bed. When a hand brushes her thigh, she shoves her knee into the person's chin. He falls on the floor. He says, "I didn't know you were awake." It's the voice of the first mate.

"That's some story you have," he says.

"It doesn't belong to me," she says.

"But you're the one telling it."

"It belongs to all of us."

"You are a strange one, aren't you?"

"You're the one trying to rape me." Miyoko swings the sun's casket into the first mate's face. He screams and retreats from the room mumbling something about being born backwards and blue.

Late one night, after Miyoko buried the heart of the girl she had been, someone knocked softly on her door. They requested Miyoko to blow out any candles that might still be burning. Visiting soldiers usually carried candles. Therefore, it was easy to know when a soldier approached, their footsteps being followed by a halo of light creeping under your door.

Tonight, there was no halo of light under the door, only the darkness and a voice requesting a darkness deeper still.

Miyoko blew out her candle. It was an order, after all.

Someone slipped through her door. This someone did not carry a candle. In the starlight, Miyoko could only see an idea of the person. Shimmering eyes. Pale skin. Clusters of hair. So much hair. Too much hair. She thought of a wisteria.

"You're a woman," Miyoko said.

"Often," said the woman.

Miyoko asked, "What do you want me to do?"

The woman said, "Listen."

The woman told Miyoko about a family of Koreans cursed to be Japanese during the day, who reverted to their true Korean nature at night. The woman told her it was a very confusing way to grow up, to be one thing in the light of day and another in the dark of night. She said she thought that's why so many Koreans had sold out their country.

"They tricked my father," Miyoko said, feeling, as she said it, a rustle of dry leaves in her chest.

"It's possible," the woman said. "Did your father receive any money for you?"

"Yes."

"Then maybe he wasn't tricked."

"How did you come to be a part of the Japanese army?" Miyoko said.

"How did you?" the woman said.

"I'm not part of the army," Miyoko said.

"But you're here," the woman said.

"Not by choice."

"Why do you think I'm a member of the army?"

"Because you're here," Miyoko said.

"Who I am has nothing to do with where I am," said the woman. She smelled like cherry blossoms. Miyoko remembered the violent, sad soldier who visited her sometimes. A crow landed on the chestnut tree outside Miyoko's window. It crowed about things.

A halo of light blossomed under Miyoko's door.

"Someone's here," she said.

The woman hid under her bed. The door opened. Aki stood there, suspicious, his face floating in a frayed bubble of candlelight.

The next night, the woman returned. Miyoko looked deep into her eyes, wondering at what to believe. She asked the woman if she could help her escape. The woman said it would be difficult.

"If the light of even a single candle touches me during the night," she said, "I'll turn into an onaga, a magpie, and be forced to fly with the rest of my kind for a dozen years before I can return to myself."

"I'll protect you from the light," Miyoko said.

"I thought you asked me to rescue you," the woman said.

"You can't save someone without letting them save you, too," Miyoko said. "It's only fair."

The woman stared at Miyoko.

"You are a strange one, aren't you?"

"I don't know," Miyoko said. "I'm just me."

The following day lasted forever. Forests of men. Requests for her to play in the courtyard. At night, Miyoko waited for the woman, but she didn't come. She contented herself by imagining her heart safe in the soil beneath her. When it rained, she worried, but she trusted in the earth and the buried chestnut to keep her heart safe. She dreamed of digging up her heart and carrying it with her, but she waited. She didn't want to uncover her heart too soon. She couldn't afford to be the girl she had been, rushing into things with her heart wide open.

The next night, the woman still didn't come. After midnight, there were screams, calls for the station to move. Miyoko didn't know what to do and then two soldiers bashed through her door. "Come with us!" they shouted.

Miyoko fought. She scratched at their throats. She tore the chrysanthemums from their lapels. The insignias fell around her feet. She escaped, for a moment, and beneath her bed she dug for her heart. The soldiers recovered, though, and came for her. They tore at her ankles, pulled her from under the bed. On the back of the truck, Aki commented on how dirty her fingernails were. The girl tried to claw out Aki's eyes, but a soldier slammed the butt of his rifle into her cheek.

Miyoko woke in a strange bed, among different mountains, beneath the same moon. She spoke to the moon of her sadness, but the moon didn't answer. The room was very much the same. Small cot, small window, pine boards, a chamber pot. She rolled off her bed and clawed at the mud. There was no woman hiding there. No heart, either. A pain grew in her stomach. In the morning, her bones shuddered and her body expelled all the rice from the day before. She felt a heart growing inside of her. She didn't recognize its rhythm. She wondered what curse the Japanese had inflicted on her, what creature she might be transforming into. The doctors assured her that she was okay. They said a new life was growing inside of her with its own and separate heart. They held her down on her new bed and injected a poison named #606. A few hours later, they removed the thing that had been alive and was now dead. A still, stone heart in its chest. Miyoko watched through her window as they buried it without a casket among the chrysanthemums sprouting on a nearby hill.

Miyoko walks onto the deck, under the stars and the moon. The wind lifts her unbraided hair. She is older than she remembers. Time moves differently as you move through it. Years and ghosts fall like cherry blossoms, collecting on your shoulders, whispering beneath your feet. She climbs the mast and asks the moon about any strange magpies that may have flown by with a chestnut strung around its neck. She believes, after her luck with the sun, after her escape, that perhaps the moon will speak to her as it had before, when she was a child.

The moon says, "Yes, but it was some time ago, I'm afraid. For your troubles, here's a very small and magical egg which you may open when things seem hopeless, though, as they so often do.

"Also, there's land over there. Maybe you will find what you seek there."

Miyoko says, "Why do you give me symbols and riddles when all I'm searching for is my heart?"

"Human hearts are nothing if not a riddle," the moon says. "Love and hate, horror and nonsense." The moon shook its head. "And they call me crazy."

Before Miyoko gets off the boat, the captain grabs her elbow. His breath smells like sesame and salt. He says, "Forget who you were and who you are. Become someone else. Understand? No one will love a woman with a story like yours."

Miyoko says, "How can I let go of the story that tells me where I came from, and where I'm going?"

The captain shakes his head. He rubs his scar. He says, "Some stories are better forgotten."

"If I forget my story," Miyoko says, "how will I ever find my heart?"

The captain has no answer for this. "Good luck," he says.

Miyoko gets off the boat. She shows the white card with the only name she remembers to the man at the pier. He says she looks very Korean for a Japanese woman. He supposes it's hard to know sometimes.

"I am Korean," Miyoko says.

"Your name, though," the man says.

"Is my business," Miyoko says.

The man shrugs.

Miyoko hires a taxi. The driver's accent is familiar to the girl. She smells garlic and pepper and sesame. The driver asks her if she'd like to store her violin in the trunk. She says no. She says she'll hold onto it. She lies down in the backseat and fails to sleep on the way to the city. She listens to the cars shush by like leaves. She watches buildings being built around her. Time's strange waltz. Cranes lifting beams high away into the clouds. When they arrive, Miyoko asks where they are.

The driver says, "This is Seoul. Everyone knows that. Especially, Koreans." He winks at the girl as if he's playing a game with her.

"I've never been to Seoul," Miyoko says. "Only my father."

"Your father must be a very successful businessman if he traveled all the way to Seoul."

"No," Miyoko says. "My father was a farmer. He lived with his hands in the mud and his head in the clouds. He never had much luck."

The Japanese army moved backward. Miyoko moved with it. Rice and chestnuts began to run out. The trees that grew inside her withered into thin husks with brittle branches and fragile leaves. They fell apart as they tore into her. Everyone was hungry. No one was satisfied. One night, there was a knock on her door, and a familiar voice requested darkness. Miyoko did this. The woman from before entered. She sat on the bed. Outside, the cicadas sang.

She said that she had found the girl's heart. She said that she had strung it around her neck like a necklace and walked until she found her.

"Please give it back to me," Miyoko said.

"It will be safer with me don't you think?" the woman said. "You might lose it again."

"It's my heart," Miyoko said.

"Nothing remains what it was," the woman said. "I found the heart, so it's mine now. It's helpful to have a spare one."

"Give it to me," Miyoko said.

"I was only kidding," the woman said.

The woman shifted. Miyoko thought, perhaps, that the woman would give her back her heart. She thought that she would not be betrayed again. A flurry of guns and running erupted outside, though. A halo of light gathered under and pushed through Miyoko's door. There was a no-name kempei holding a gun and a candle. The candlelight touched the woman beside Miyoko. The woman burned, pale and beautiful and afraid. Her body folded and fell to pieces, blood-dark cherry blossoms gathering in a mass of feathers.

The kempei fired his pistol at the transforming woman. A wounded magpie flew out the door, carrying with it the girl's heart.

Beside Miyoko, a single, bloody feather remained. She screamed and ran at the soldier. The soldier backed away and threw down a handful of white cards.

"These are identification cards," he said. "Take them and run while you can. The Americans are coming. They will kill everything in their path. Women. Children. They won't know you are Korean. They'll assume you are Japanese. Run! Go!"

In Seoul, Miyoko sees that she and the city are older and newer than she remembers. The buildings are tall and transparent. Everyone can see inside of everywhere. Where do these people hide their secrets? Their hearts? The city's walls reflect Miyoko's face, a ghost among the forests of steel and glass. Miyoko sees that she is a woman now. A schoolgirl calls her ajumma. She tells Miyoko that she is dirty and old.

Miyoko chooses a spot in front of a giant, old bell. One place is as good as another. She removes her violin, laying the open case, like a casket, at her feet. She plays the music she has composed during the journey to find her lost heart.

Moving on has many costs.

This is how Miyoko has traveled, all these months, all these years, from the time and place where her heart flew away, to the time and place where she boarded the ship with its old and wiry captain.

Some of Seoul's citizens ignore her, their eyes sliding away. Some stand and watch. A few offer payment for whatever they hear in the songs. Beauty. Sadness. Inspiration. Comfort. Miyoko cannot choose how people hear the songs that she plays, anymore than she can control the changing nature of her feelings about them. Some days it is all-consuming hatred. Some days the sky is blue and the rain a startling bliss. The truth is that she has found her life means something new every day, and so it is with the music she plays. She cannot say where her heart will lead her next. She can only choose whether to see and to listen, whether to follow, or not.

The city is full of coffee shops in which there are woman dressed in short skirts and dark stockings. Miyoko does not understand. She sits in a cafe and drinks a coffee with too much sugar and a design on top, drawn with milk, that resembles a sesame leaf. Miyoko asks where the trees have gone and people direct her to the national forest. There, she sits under a pine tree and shivers in the memory of the man who wanted and wanted. She asks the wind if he knows where the magpie who carries her heart has gone. The wind says, "I've seen the magpie of which you speak. It's flown to the East Sea and has become a woman again, for the dozen years are over. The woman is now in the midst of a battle against my brother the sea, who's really just another woman suffering under an evil enchantment.

"Things will be what they will be, I'm afraid," the wind says. "When you reach the beach, remove a tooth from your own gums. Bury this tooth and an army will come to your aid. Take the woman who stole your heart and do what you must, or what you choose, whichever seems easiest or best."

Miyoko hardly believes she has been wandering and playing her music for twelve years. She boards a bus at the East Seoul Bus Station and travels to the East Sea. She travels by train the last part of the way. As the sun rises, flashing along the cliffs and the rails, she asks where so much time has gone, and what, in it's leavetaking, it has done with the girl, with her heart, with her country. She wonders how so much time could have been lost in the journey back to herself. Maybe it will be too late. Maybe it has always been too late. Perhaps, as soon as Aki's hand found hers, time had already won.

Time answers Miyoko. Time says, "I don't know. Maybe with the proper distance, with a telescope or fairy tale, you could see that everything still exists inside of everything else. But telescopes and fairy tales belong to men. Not so much to me."

Miyoko finds it strange that she doesn't find it strange that time, and the sun, and the moon, and the wind speak with her. She supposes that they speak to everyone, if they care to listen. Perhaps, she thinks, there are benefits to carrying silence within your chest.

On the beach, near her home, she finds no sign of her former home or even the village. There are lobster restaurants and wi-fi parks. So many people in black-and-white stripes. She finds her way to the sea and sees everything as the wind described. The woman who ran away with Miyoko's heart battles for her life against the sea, punching and kicking.

Miyoko reaches a hand into her mouth, preparing to pull free a tooth, to create another hole inside herself. She imagines planting the tooth, stained with her own blood, among seashells and sand. An army of soldiers would rise, the wind said.

Miyoko watches the sea and the woman do battle. The woman looks so much older than Miyoko remembers. It looks like she is swimming, and that she is happy.

Everything, Miyoko supposes, looks like war from a certain perspective. She removes the moon's egg from her bag and buries it beneath the sand, hoping that the tide might sweep the child back, with time, to its mother.

She waits for the magpie woman to climb free of the sea. Her hair is dark and wet and dripping. Pearls of water glisten on her shoulders. A scar darkens the skin above her right hip, a wound that time, it seems, refused to heal.

There is nothing hanging around the woman's neck.

"Ssibal," Miyoko says.

"I couldn't carry your heart any longer. I'm sorry. It got too heavy."

"Where is it?" Miyoko asks.

"That way," the woman says, pointing north. "I wanted to plant it somewhere far away from your pain."

"This is my home," Miyoko says. "Or, at least, it was."

"I didn't know that," the woman says.

Miyoko walks north, playing and singing, until, in front of her, beneath a bright and empty blue sky, among the hills that lie between the city's new skyscrapers, she sees a chestnut tree, old, wide, and low-branching. Loud with cicadas and beautiful with yellow blossoms. It shouldn't be so beautiful, but, it is. On a blanket, there is another woman. Miyoko recognizes the woman, but she doesn't believe it. Children play around her, running around the tree trunk, punching each other in the arm. One is a boy, and one is a girl.

"Hello," the woman says, studying Miyoko. "You look familiar."

"Hello," Miyoko says.

A man is selling pretzels nearby. Another man is playing his saxophone. The pretzels smell of salt and fat. The saxophone sings of mud and clouds.

"Is your father here?" Miyoko says.

"My father died several years ago. We buried him near this tree. He loved chestnuts."

Miyoko looks at the ground under her feet. She looks at the chestnut tree. "I'm sorry to hear that." She steps into the shade of the tree, of her tree, and feels sheltered and trapped, the rustle of the leaves, the wash of sun and shadow, her father's bones beneath her feet.

"Thank you," the woman says.

Miyoko wraps her arms around the tree and presses her ear against the bark. Columns of black ants march past, burrowing in and out of the wood. The wood tickles Miyoko's ear. She remembers the forest that grew inside of her, the trail of blood, the magic that surrounded and still surrounds her heart. Everything has grown together, it seems, inside of her and the earth. She doesn't know what to make of the past, present, or future. Names seem superfluous at this point.

"Ajumma?" the woman says.

Miyoko doesn't answer. She holds tight to this tree, grown wild and strange with life. The history of everything seems within reach. All of the amalgamations. All of the contradictions. In the earth. In the tree. In her heart. Love and hate and horror and nonsense. For a moment, she can hear the music to which time dances. Car horns and windblown leaves. Pounding jackhammers and the waking scream of locusts. Footsteps in the snow. Branches against a window.

The woman puts her hand on Miyoko's shoulder.

"Little sister?"

Miyoko doesn't respond. Not yet. She listens. She remembers. In spite of everything. Because of everything.

 TRICIA KNOLL

THE FATES' TRIFECTA

The Fates play cards as dusk releases into night,
a game of war with decks of face cards and jokers.
One proposes to the other two, for a challenge,
that each tell a story that folds together unlike things
that come in threes. The best wins bragging rights.
If a tie, to pass the night an extra gulp each of vodka
infused with blood oranges and passion fruit.

The first said spoons coddle blind mice,
cutlery is heavy-handled, but forks—
not those with slim tines for fruit or pork
or how trails divide in the woods to offer
choice. Ah, forks! She raised jags of lightning,
branched after-images, the zing of oxygen
rearranged as ozone, ragged memories of plasma
for a mirage glimpse of far-off hills.

The second invoked the End of Day circus
under a red, yellow and blue striped tent.
In the center ring Cerberus walks on hind feet
since his contract ended to guard hell, too many
inmate escapes. He struts to show off his heads
in tricorn hats. In the equestrian ring
white stallions canter below muscular women
in silver sequins carrying snowy owls.
Behind a veil of mist, in the north circle,
a procession of the lost and abandoned
with spotted hides walk in step
three-by-three to Bach's Air on a G String.

The third Fate spoke low. Prophets say they see
the future. Few hear it through their ossicles
—hammer, anvil, stirrup—gifts that should
deliver both slurred and overheard evil
to the open window of the ear. This is why,
she says, for seers who refuse to pay heed, she grabs
gold scissors, cuts foolscap bond scribbled
with oracle poems, and folds their bones
into a packet tied with braids of silver silk, sweet grass,
and red wool yarn to tuck beside their headstones.
May they learn to hear warnings of treachery.

Tipples to a tie—spirit, blood and passion—
then Fates turn to spin their work this night.

# JAMES GRABILL

BOTTLENECK

At the blazingly rich entrance to eternity, the build-up stands shoulder-to-shoulder in the lobby of timelessness, throwing its relative lack of weight into attempts to transact at the rococo transom before entering the great superconscious choral halls. Having outdone ourselves here, we're over a generation behind up there with all the Chinese dinner jackets, fox-body stoles and tropical raingear, the Philippine bullet belts, black and yellow city running shoes, pilgrim-buckle grandma's galoshes, the many pointy-toed hard-nailed tango heels and you name it.

From the gates to the quasi-spatial peripheries, the effects there are inseparable from great numbers of recently departed souls each with sets of salt and pepper shakers, where the decks are now mixed, minus a few royal families, with everyone who lacks substance milling around on cloud barges, a few lugging along euphonium cases or shopping bags with grapefruit and tuna or blue-violet knit snowflake mittens for anticipated grandchildren. It's one deceased recollection of having been alive then the next, floating in from a snapped fuselage or undisclosed riparian overgrowth, one a time arriving in a nude Parisian hair net or red undies or with an untied velvetine ribbon.

The reports have it so many are waiting, whispering at once of their late experiences live in 7th floor business English, Latvian, heavy Argentinian script, Jesuit Latin, or vocal Kiowa, as light pinwheels in the ten million directions after surfacing in salt-sea swells off the Iberian Peninsula or from a heated-up mating retreat on a Miami cove, or off gold-trimmed eaves of a Cambodian jungle temple, or after falling through crisp Olympic rings of hand-rubbed ritual meditation skulls, where the massive congestion everywhere at once makes new arrivals more humble.

Study #2 for The Sticks

SAMANTHA EDMONDS

MAMA SAYS

Blood on white underwear. Mama says: Take it to the river. Be home before dark. Washing songs, icy hands. Blood in the water. Moonman in the bushes. You're a good girl. Polite. You smile at him. You have never been this close to him before. A story in the trees, older than your lifetime. Fearfully whispered about. Evening sunlight dapples the grass. Moonman won't come out. Long-toothed, shaggy-headed, hairy-knuckled, yellow-eyed. The middle fingers on both his hands are the same length. You understand him now. Tell him: don't be frightened. Sunrays are just moonlight before it's reflected. You show him your underwear, explain to him that starting today you too are slave to a lunar cycle. We're just like the oceans, you say.

Backaches under scratchy sheets. Mama says: Say your prayers. Good night. Moonbeams come in like swords on your bed. You sit up. Your stomach cramps. You were not able to get the underwear clean. Instead of brilliant red, the stain is dirty brown. This color is more shameful than the first—and less vibrant. When you open your mouth to God, Moonman answers outside. He's talking to the sky, too. There is something inside a part of you that has never been entered before.

The blood dries up. Mama says: Count the days. Pay attention. The nights come sooner, so that now on your way home from school, or soccer practice, or Grandmother's house, you are walking in the dark. Easy to get lost. Easier not to. Dusty paths worn from years of footprints guide you, so that every branch cracked under your boots is expected. The moon, once plump, goes missing in slices, like a bread loaf. Moonman wanes, too. Thinner, transparent. You can see the muscle in his legs, the claws of his fingers. But soft stuff, too. Heart behind ribcage. Tissue and tendon, easy to tear. All the tiny bones, like pieces of space rock, that make up a spine, that wiggle toes. He walks you home every day. Says words you've never heard: Lunation. Gibbous. Give him some new words of your own: Follicular. Endometrium. Touch your fingers to his mouth. Put his in your mouth. Share the same insides. Love is when even the blood and bones are precious to you.

Full dark, no stars. Moonman is invisible, if he was ever there at all. Mama says: Stop talking nonsense. You're too old for games.

Ovulation day. Mama says: It will hurt like this every month for the rest of your life. Don't worry. But something inside you that was never alive is dying even as you breathe. In the woods, Moonman has come back in stages, a pinky finger, a single ear, one leg. From your bedroom window, inventory the parts of him as they reappear. He can smell the blood before it's out of you. His nose quivers against glass. Fogs it. You quiver, too. Without you telling him he knows he was missed.

Blood spots on black underwear, hardly noticeable. Mama says: Bad girl. I told you to count. That was your last clean pair. At the river without permission. Moonlight breaks through tree cracks, splinters the dirt trail. Step on a crack, break your mama's back. Sunlight will call you home. Mama will call you bad. Every month will call this out of you, control you, unless you find a place where the cycle doesn't restart. Where the night goes on, the darkness uninterrupted. Moonman is there, fully formed and waiting.

Blood on sticky skin, pale thighs. Free-bleeding. Who cares what Mama says. Throw back your head and howl. Tonight you are holding nothing in.

# Tobias Peterson

TWO POEMS

FABLE

A few of us, woodish things, went venturing
bankward to the water. Crows sprung
from driftwood and a blue salmon
skull. Pine sap gummed our neck
fur into bristles

                      until the river's scent
was lost to us, who leaned there peering down
a greengray passage, the sturgeon's low heaven.
She hovers in her bed and bats her lids, beyond time.

Our island was a ship speeding over
the dappled plateaus of her.
There in the glassy depths
she whiskered the current
with four fleshy wands of divining.
We bent to parse pebble light
from her wink of intention.

The crows arrayed among the far
cedars, according to her glances.
We bellowed for knowing, tossed down
stones, a salmon skull, but the birds
were now patches of dark in the wood.

The sturgeon closed and opened her golden eye
and they were gestures of ink.

WOLF MUSIC

Sleep until your tribe
From the other side of heaven
Wakes you with baying.
                —Vasko Popa

Though their wet skins pressed
our shoulders, we found
that we loved the things we had killed
in the wild. In the clearing beyond
the fort, we watched their grimfaced
waltzes, the distance of locked arms.

We winnowed our voices to lines
or half-circles. To hear them
the crows shook themselves in the rain.
We took turns waving words
across the bank and pricked our ears
to the east. The river filled
with muscled white flashing.

    There, we said, before we knew
to point, before we knew to dry their guts
into musical string. *There*, we fashioned
second bodies and mimicked their loping
rhythms down the green hill. There
our tongues danced at the corners of our smiling.

DELIA GARIGAN

TWO POEMS

FOX TIDE

Oysters underfoot in the voiceless dark
filter and pulse like living stones.
Their tide draws the forest down
into the inlet, bites the land away.

I crouch along the water, and the fox
crouches too. Red as memory in my arms,
and as rough. He stinks like more than a man,
his tongue and teeth a promise of dizzying sin.

The forest door is flung aside;
a roadway of light sings over the water.
How many more times will I be opened?
He turns and in a movement, slices.

Blood ranges black over the rocks,
draining into cracks and sand.
Golden fleets of moon-shard signal to shore, but
our light has dissolved   into the oysters' ready flesh.

NIGHT TRAIN

Frost sparks across the fields, and
a distant fringe of woodland goes sliding into dream.
Two little-girl shoes slither her back
against the seat. The cigar box tight on
her lap slides a weary sigh. The dark
perfumed ladies' murmur feathers
through the dim-lit passage.
Three blue beads knock together there
in furtive chatter with unwound watch that stayed
when Father was taken.
Dusted by a dim bird's wing in empty flight.
Larval jaws sever the silence; a beetle's clattering carapace
rings musty emptiness. Hours run that must not be touched;
they gleam through the wheels' unrelenting mutter.
Gaslight on the upswept hair. The brakes' soft squealing;
the train pulls into town. She lifts the cover.

JOHN A. McDERMOTT

A ROUX IS A REDUCTION

The shredder is squat, about a foot and a half high. It cost Jason thirty dollars at the office store. It's dark gray on the bottom—really just a waste basket—and the top, where the spool of teeth wait, is lighter gray. Its black electrical cord is short, only a yard or so long with a two-prong plug, but the power strip under the desk is near where Jason sits cross-legged on the wood floor of his study. He's on the north side of the house; the bedrooms, the one he shares with his wife, Amy, and the baby's room next to that, are on the second floor of the south end. Between them lay the dining room, the kitchen, the living room, a flight of stairs and a short hallway.

It's nearly midnight and Amy's been asleep since after the ten o'clock news (it was a day sponsored by F: flood, famine, fire. Yesterday was brought to them by B: burglary, beatings, billionaires. He knows the last thing doesn't seem to fit the list, but really, billionaires are a crime, aren't they? Perhaps tomorrow will be another W day: war, war, war. That seems a common letter lately.) So Amy went to bed, wondering aloud for the fiftieth time of their marriage why they watch the news when it's never good. Jason says, again, a response they both know he's going to, has to, give: it's our responsibility to be informed. Good citizens know what's going on. And that's why they subscribe to the local paper, a regional paper, and *The New York Times* on Sundays, though Jason reads it online everyday. He likes to be current. (They are a thousand miles from New York City. Sometimes that seems safe; sometimes it feels like banishment. They are both originally from upstate, but moved south, way south, for work.)

But there's this thing about some information: Jason needs to dispose of it. In the right way, the sensible way. Bank statements, mortgage receipts, those checks the credit card companies send them both that could so easily be endorsed by a thief, or more likely, if they succumb to temptation, endorsed by themselves. All of these papers need to be destroyed. Hence the thirty dollar shredder, plugged in by its short cord to the power strip under the desk, its green light glowing and its mouth ready to rumble. It churns like the purr of a mechanical cat. Jason usually shreds during the day, never when Amy's asleep, but the bedroom door is shut and she has the overhead fan twirling—it's a hot, humid East Texas night and air conditioning only does so much in their poorly insulated fixer-upper with its single pane glass and gaps at every window sill and door frame. Heat escapes in winter, cool in summer. The house is an environmental nightmare, its carbon footprint Sasquatchian.

Jason squirms just thinking about it, sitting there on the floor on a Tuesday night. Almost Wednesday. Jason hates the house. Hates mowing the yard, hates cleaning the gutters. Hates trimming bushes and worrying about the termites and the roaches and the red ants. He misses their cramped two-bedroom apartment in Albany where they belong. No yard work. If something was wrong, he called the landlord. He tries to remember homeownership saves money, but it's a trick, a task. His brother, the businessman, tells him rent is throwing money away. Jason throws other things away now that he owns a home. Time. And paper. But he shreds them both first.

The machine will only take six pages at once or it jams. He knows when it's going to jam because the growl gets lower, decidedly bass, and slows down, as if it had indigestion. Then he has to hit the reverse button and unfeed the mess. He pulls out fringed documents—Department of Transportation plate renewal notices and cable bill receipts and come-ons for loans, loans from every source possible, with interest rates higher than his age (Jason is twenty-nine), and medical forms and page after page from hospitals and labs that say in bold print at the top THIS IS NOT A BILL but clearly is the forerunner of A BILL and given enough time and insurance company denials will become A BILL. He shreds those warning notices. He pays the bills. He wishes he could shred those too but he and Amy have good credit. Their numbers are high. They are responsible citizens. They are informed. They are current. They are trying to save this house. They tried to start a family. They are trying to be diligent. They are drowning.

Jason shreds bank statements from a year ago. He always waits a while before he gets rid of those, in case there's a problem, though he knows the bank has records and must keep a long computerized history of his account. The green and white logoed paper goes through gracefully; the shredder happily chews its opening course. Jason is careful to slip only a few pages in at a time. He doesn't want to discourage it. A friend once had a shredder burst into flame on him—Jason hates that story. Coffee pots melt down, toasters start fires, shredders explode. He doesn't trust the implements of modern life, but he's addicted to coffee, likes toast and jam, needs to shred. Must shred. It's an addiction. It's like other cleansing rituals, yoga, spas, purges. Jason, though he hasn't told Amy, would shred everything in this life if he could. Their temperamental car, their furniture (too much, too big, too trendy), their groceries, and their clothes. Their cds—music, not bonds.

Their magazine subscriptions and the work they bring home with them. He's a salesman, she's a community college instructor. Papers to grade, blue book exams. Contracts. Travel vouchers. More receipts. Always receipts.

He shreds a sheaf of carbonless, duplicate checks, the wispy white paper with ghostly blue amounts from long-ago purchases. These are from when they first moved to Texas, three years ago. First water bills. First cable bills. First phone and electric and gas bills. Ancient checks are a history, a diary. But they shred easily, the equivalent of fine baby hair in the paper world. Like gossamer, Jason thinks, whatever gossamer is. He knows it's frail and thin. Angels' wings are always gossamer. He has no clue what gossamer really is. He wonders if it's made from geese. No, he supposes, that would be goosamer. A children's word. He's so tired. The light in the study is dim. The small green panel light burns like an alien's eye. The machine spins, a curved cylinder of incisors. Maybe canines. No: fangs.

Jason gets careless. He thrusts a thick wad of hotel bills down the gullet. The machine coughs, but keeps eating. Not from last spring's family visits, though many had stayed in the same hotel. They paid their own way; nobody wanted to ask for help on that kind of trip. It was an obligation. No one wanted to come, everyone did. No, these were more recent, from the nights Amy spent downtown, out of the house. There were more than a few when she couldn't handle it. Or maybe him. Or maybe the quiet. Jason stuffs in a few more statements. *Thank You For Your Stay.* "Stay" used to mean stop, he'd just recently learned. Stay! Not just like a dog, frozen, but really stopped. Cease! Desist! Stay! *Thank you for your recent cease.* He doesn't want to stay. He wants to cease.

There's a section of the morning paper in a basket within arm's reach. He tries to cram the front page in the shredder, but it takes a couple tries. The headline *More Die in Middle East* keeps sticking. He reverses, it sticks again. The machine groans, but finally eats it all. He tosses the rest of the section aside and reaches for some junk mail. Blow-in cards and flyers. He holds the envelope from a mail-order gift Amy had bought him within the last week. The pale green paper has a white border and black printing: *Don't ruin your surprise: Open your gift before this envelope.* The gift was a book. A bestseller about love and grief and rekindling romance. This came after the nights in the hotel. The nights he stayed behind and manned the house. In case it burned down. In case someone called. In case something needed shredding. The envelope had contained the shipping statement. Ah, yes: had he peeked, he would have discovered what was beneath the matching wrapping paper: HEALING HANDS, HEALING HEARTS. Ordered 7/9, shipped 7/11. It would have given away the surprise. The surprise that she'd sent him a gift? That she wanted to heal? That someone thought there was a cure? That a thin, hardcover book could promise that much? That hands had anything to do with it? He looks at the envelope clutched in his hands and stuffs it through and it's gone. No more warning. Don't ruin your surprise. His legs cramp and he stands and stretches. The machine waits, humming and satisfied, but willing to devour more. He sees the book. It's on his cluttered desk. He holds it above the machine and wonders.

The dust jacket is nothing; skinny, shiny, slick. An oily appetizer. The cover is a different matter, hard and brittle. Like eating bone. But the shredder does it with grace. No wheezing, no smoke, no problem. The six sheet limit...suspends. The machine willingly takes seven, eight pages, then whole chapters. The mouth gets wider. Jason watches the churning teeth, revolving, revolting, they mesmerize him like ocean waves. Sailors lulled by the water throw themselves overboard. Jason wants to reach in and touch the shining metal. He hovers, his hand above the lip. His fingers wouldn't fit, far fatter than six pages. And the pain: he considers the sensation of cuts, the tearing, searing, the teeth could do. He shudders. But still.

He reaches for a magazine. The cover story is about the price of gas. Jason wants a hybrid, but they still owe thousands on their current car, bought for its roominess—space for a child seat, space for diaper bags and toys. They don't need the space. The car seat is empty in the hall. The diaper bag is spotless, as pristine as it was from the factory in China. The baby came but left as babies sometimes do: silently, without much fuss, but leaving a swath of pain in its short and narrow path. The machine eats the magazine and gulps and burps and asks for more.

Jason wants to jam the car seat in the shredder. He wants to start getting rid of all of the baby's things. The baby's name was William. He would start with that. He finds a receipt marked clearly with William's name at the top of the page. Birthdate. Mother's maiden name. Jason holds it lightly in both hands and lets it slide into the maw. He sees *W* and *LL* and *M* chewed and knows it fell somewhere in the basket. He shreds every medical notice he can find. An entire manila envelope of them. He moves on to newspaper articles. Shock. Community sadness. Obituaries. He runs out of paper. He goes to the closet and finds the blanket. Soft, light blue, dryer sheet scented like sugar and cream. The machine shreds it all the same, only a few pale threads left hanging on the blades. Jason sneaks down the back hall and gets the car seat. It's still brand new. It's hard beige plastic and cushiony man-made fibers. The shredder slices it into so many bits. The basket should be overflowing, but it's not. It's all settling so neatly, tidily, like a box of cereal four inches from the sealed, seamed cellophane top. Contents may have settled during shipping, Jason remembers. The contents are settling.

He stuffs diapers and teddy bears and then another box of old bank statements. The car loan. His last month's sales charts. All of this clutter. It's getting smaller and smaller, and so much more manageable. If he had known how easy this was, he would have done it a lot sooner. He pushes down another book. Pictures of Amy pregnant. An old calendar. The phone. He doesn't mean to do that, but it was in easy reach and he's in a rush and it's going down so smoothly. He feels bad about it, but Amy has a cell and she hardly ever uses it, the rollover minutes pile up behind her, and now she can just dip into that savings. They don't need a land-line. Or an answering machine. Or a television. A DVD player. The radio in the kitchen. The oversized clock in the hall. He reads the big face before it disappears. 4:14. It seems he'd only started a minute ago. Where had the time gone?

Down the hole, sliced up, and neatly tumbling.

He considers Amy's cookbooks, volumes lined up on the pantry shelves. He goes to the kitchen and finds one, the biggest. He remembers her using it last winter, her apron extended over her heavy belly. She was flour-speckled and laughing. She said she was making a roux. He didn't know what that meant.

"A roux is a reduction," she told him. She stirred with a long handled wooden spoon. "The trick is to thicken the sauce, but not to make it heavy. You're left with just what you need."

"I thought a rue was a street," he said, picking at the black olives she'd left on the table. She held open her mouth and he fed her one. They kissed, a salty peck.

"Different spelling," she says, then, her voice mock-tragic: "It can also mean regret. I regret to tell you. I'm besot with rue."

"So if I have this sauce I'll be rueful," Jason says.

"No, you'll be roux-full."

"This is all so confusing."

"It's just a trick," she laughed. "A ruse."

He puts the cookbook back. It's too much to handle. For now. He casts about for something else, but he can't do Amy's things without her permission. He can't shred her gym bag or her walking shoes or her bicycle. The wheels would fit, the seat would, too. He wanders back to the machine and stands above it, cheeks flushed, still the urge to stuff things between the blades so strong, so strong. He feels the lip of the mouth with his fingertips. It's the slightest bit warm. He's put it through the paces and it's a real thoroughbred. He can't believe he ever thought this shredder would let him down. He looks down into the basket, looks down, sees a black hole, and sees his name. William is down there, too. He can read it. A *W* and *LL* and an *M*. He's sure that's what is says. Then Jason again. Jason. Jason. He reaches out to touch it, touch the letters. He hardly remembers it any more. He remembers when Amy used to say it often. Jason. William. Stay. The letters disperse, like shimmering water, only so much confetti. He moves forward and falls.

The machine accepts him.

Jason is reduced and he revels in his new form: thin strips of him, slivers, long lean slices that curl on both ends. There's no blood and there's no pain. It's a very clean process. He feels recycled. Reborn. The strands of him mingle easily with the rest of the jetsam of his modern married life: bills, pitches, receipts, lures, grievances, and grief. He feels lighter, calmer; the basket is dark and cozy, the heat from the engine above him filters down like an incubator's lamp. Perhaps he is a chick now and will grow into something new, something sturdier. Or maybe he'll remain weightless forever. He's warm and if he still had a mouth he'd smile, the first time in a long time.

But there's no one in the study to flip the *off* button and he worries about the current. He doesn't want to burn the house down. Yet the worry passes. Everything will be fine. The shredder's green eye will glow all night, unblinking, until Amy comes down in the morning, looking for her husband, checking room to room, calling his name, like she used to, and Jason will be there. He just can't speak. He's there in the bottom of the basket, still in strips, bits and pieces, unable to utter a word. He can't call her name, and he'd like to, but it's not really a burden: he's lighter now, at last—reduced, not thick, what's left is only what is essential—he's lighter now at last.

 KURT LUCHS

NATURAL HISTORY

I.
Today we studied the ruins.
Your eyelashes were already a legend among the Byzantines.
Once, I believed you could read the stars,
perhaps even read your own mind.
Yet you can't feel your own grave
rushing at you with its mouth open,
the branches of that place soaked in a green light,
the clenched teeth of the moon.

II.
That was some of the work I did for extra credit.

Then they made me chalk your name
a hundred times on the blackboard;
but the thought of there being so many of you,
each one the same,
each dotting her "i" with a drop of blood...
It was too much. I flinched
and hooded the blackboard with a hospital sheet.

III.
In the shorn fields
Death gathers a bouquet
of all the hands that ever touched you.

IV.
Ladies and gentlemen, my latest discovery:
the heart is a piece of coal.

Yes, a piece of coal in which the fossilized leaves
of an extinct fern
are just beginning to stir from a breeze that passed
centuries ago.
If you look closely,
at the tip of the branch is poised
an impossibly small bird, with hollow sockets that look
neither left nor right.
The bird, also, is extinct.

DEVON BALWIT

TWO POEMS

A RICTUS MISTAKEN FOR PAIN
(after Jonas Burgert's Zyklus-Potsdam Tryptich, 2006)

The eagle-headed gods
    demand propitiation,

but ignore the proffered
    first fruits, the pulse

of upturned throats. Their shrieking
    crumbles plaster

as clown-priests exhort the broken,
    staff and stole

whetting a serrated horizon. You bow
    but cannot hide

impenitence. Soon their obsidian blades
    will snag your heart

for the dark urn, your death rictus
    mistaken for pain.

You, however, will know it a mask
    of deepest satisfaction.

VISITATION

faceless comes the boneman

>sack slung over his shoulder

each step roiling burlap

>a hap of femur and humerus

great tubercule and capitulum

>out-poking like your face

peeking to glimpse dread

>pocketing it as you do a marble

to roll later between fingerpads

>as adults weary you with trivia

while ignoring the terrors

>just beneath its skin

the boneman's cape tatters

>as he walks gusting a dry leaf rustle

you will later mimic to your

>friends a runty mockingbird seeking

a laugh while secretly your heart

>thunders in your throat

at the emptiness wafting

>in the wake of his passing

Jennifer Pullen

WINGS AND WIRES

I

Icarus sits in the clock tower and runs handfuls of sand over the rusting gears so as to burnish them to copper and bronze again. He loves the gears and wishes they would work, make the hands of the clock go around and mark the time. His father tells him stories about how, before the flood, the clock tower used to sit in the center of a great square and chime the hour, and everyone knew that two o'clock meant that ships would be docking bringing treasures from Mars and beyond. Icarus wishes he lived in a time which still had a use for a clock. Now time lacks hours and only has dawn and dark. Light or the absence of light are the only measure and the only meaning. Now the clock tower is just one more tower jutting out of the water and pushing towards the sky.

Finished with shining the gears, Icarus delays heading down the moist stone steps and instead stares out at the all-encompassing sea. He watches the waves rise and fall, shaping a false cartography. He imagines valleys, mountains, and meadows covered in green grass. If he lets his eyes fall half shut he can almost fool himself that the blue green water shifts into a rippling plain. His father calls such games foolish, says he can't ever mistake the damned water for anything but a curse, and that Icarus should stop mooning around. Icarus sighs and looks away from the water and up toward the sun. He sees a pelican silhouetted there, and he envies the bird its flight and mobility as well as its ability to live despite the encroaching waters. He wonders if pelicans resemble turkeys. His father has told him about turkeys, about Thanksgiving, about everyone eating until they were fit to burst. But turkeys are among the things (including grass) that Icarus has no memory of ever seeing. He squints into the sun and stretches out his arms. He names himself a pelican and imagines swooping into the water to catch a fish and then rising back up again.

He hears his father's voice echoing across the waves, and suddenly he's just a boy again, and he heads towards the stairs. He doesn't want his father to see his secret place inside the clock tower.

II

Icarus asks his father to tell him about the flood. Only stories of disaster make him believe in the world his father claims to have lived in. He sits behind his father in the row boat, watches his father's back move, so strong, muscles clenching and unclenching as he rows. In the distance he can see one of the towers (his father says they used to be called skyscrapers), the one that the sea-gulls nest on. He braces himself for the act of gathering eggs. He hates it. His father snorts.

"Once upon a time, the flood covered everything with water, the end," he says.

Icarus tries again, asks his father to tell him about the stars, about how in space everything is at once perpetual night and endless sources of light burning in the sky. His father doesn't respond. Sometimes, to get his father to tell a story, he has to ask multiple questions. Somedays, his father doesn't want to talk. Icarus already knows most of the stories, but he wants to hear them anyway.

"Tell me the one about your job again," he says. The word *job* tastes strange and foreign in his mouth. Once his father showed him a piece of money, said people used to go to work for money, and then buy food with it. Icarus thought this was hilarious, since work was what one did to find food, not to get pieces of soggy paper.

His father keeps rowing and the tower seems to float disembodied in the water, never getting any closer or farther away. The air tastes of salt.

Icarus waits, because he's learned that stories can take time to ripen.

"Drop the net," his father says, "dredge for sea-weed. We need our greens."

Icarus drops the weighted net and holds onto the rope. He waits. The story rises from his father's lips.

"Back before the damned ocean ate everything, I used to fly in a space-ship that could go beyond the sun and out of the atmosphere of earth, but my crew and I could still breathe, because that ship was better than this rickety boat by far. I was often gone for months or even years at a time, exploring. It made your mother angry, but I kept going, because it was my job to try to find us other places to live. Because you see, we'd used up most of the earth, overflowed Mars, and the other planets were already inhabited by hostile indigenous life-forms. So I and hundreds of others like me were sifting through the universe the way one would sift through flour or sand, looking for things out of place."

Icarus opens his mouth to ask a question, and his father cuts him off.

"I know you don't know about flour, so just trust me. I looked and looked and looked, because I and a few others like me knew that the earth had an expiration date."

Icarus had actually intended to ask what happened to the people on Mars, but the words *expiration date* draws his attention, and so he doesn't. Also, he gets the feeling his first question would have been somehow hurtful. Once, he asked his father to tell him about his mother, about the day they got married. His father had told the story, but later that night, Icarus heard his father crying softly. He'd pretended to still be asleep. Another time, he'd asked what happened to all the other people, and his father hadn't spoken for days.

"What is an expiration date?"

"Stop asking questions. You wanted a story, so let me tell it. So, we were running out of time. I used to long for the taste of fresh air or the feel of the bark of a tree under my hand, but I told myself it would all be worth it if I could just find a new place for humanity. Your mother was beautiful. She had red hair, like you, and freckles all over her nose. She laughed a lot, and saved her tears until I was asleep, because she knew what I was doing was important. Her work was important too. She was a scientist, trying to figure out how to make plants grow on ships out in space, so that if we had to we could live indefinitely amongst the stars. She used to carry your baby self on her back while she worked. She had a white coat. When I came back from searching the last time and visited her at work, she'd had a break-through. She was excited, despite the storms, despite the warnings about severe weather. She ran out to her lab to get a plant sample. Then the flood came, and I picked you up and climbed to the top of the big bio-tech company's skyscraper. I watched the water come."

When his father's voice goes still and only the sound of water testing the edges of the boat and the cries of the gulls remain, Icarus pulls in the net and dumps out a clump of slimy green seaweed, and then drops it onto the floor of the boat. Dinner. He releases the net into the water again and looks from his father's muscled back to the sky and the gulls riding the wind. He wishes he were older, not just thirteen, that his body wasn't still growing and his limbs weren't long and thin. Then he could row as well as his father without getting in the way. Then maybe they could row so fast they'd find land somewhere, and his mother would be there, a plant and soil cupped in her hands. She'd hold out her hands to him and say, *Here, this is for you.*

But adulthood seems so far away, and his father says there is no more dry land, only a few birds, the fish, and maybe a handful of other unfortunate souls holed up in skyscrapers somewhere. Once he asked his father about mountains (he saw some in a soggy old picture book once) and his father says no, all leveled for minerals. Icarus didn't ask any more questions about mountains. He thinks of the birds, of his father's stories about traveling into the night sky, and he decides that wings would really be the things to have, the only way to escape and see something other than water water everywhere.

"Escape isn't possible," his father says. He looks over his shoulder at Icarus, who tries to look small, to look like someone who would never dream of something impossible.

"Where would I go?" Icarus asks.

"Good question." His father goes back to rowing. The tiny waves slap the edge of the boat, and out in the distance a whale's spout breaks the monotony of the horizon. Once his father told him that whale mothers stay with their babies for only a year, but when the calf is first born, all of the adults in the pod push it towards the surface and teach it to breathe.

#

Once they arrive at the tower of gulls, they tie the boat up to a protruding window frame and step through the window and inside. Icarus likes the clock tower better than the skyscrapers, preferring damp stone to smelly rotting carpets. But he doesn't voice his preference, since his father thinks that his obsession with the old time-keeping device displays foolishness. They climb stair after stair, and Icarus feels his legs burn, his muscles protest. He wishes again for wings, or that one of the elevators that used to carry people to the top still worked.

On the roof they gather eggs, stepping around bird shit and bits of broken glass. The gulls dive at their heads and try to chase the humans away from their nests made from dried sea-weed and human detritus. Grabbing for an egg, dodging a pecking beak and angry yellow eyes, Icarus catches a glimpse of water-soaked paper covered in words, and the red sleeve of a shirt. He hates the birds for a moment for taking these hints of the past for themselves. One bird pecks him, and then another and another as he goes from nest to nest. His hands bleed but he only winces and then continues because he knows that without eggs he and his father will have to eat only sea-weed for dinner. He's careful to take only one egg from each nest. His father says that they have to leave enough eggs so that some will hatch and turn into more sea-gulls. The carry-sack made from an old jacket sags with eggs, and his father takes it, says it's too heavy for a boy. As his father turns to leave Icarus snatches up a handful of shed feathers from the ground. He glares at the birds, and thinks that if they can have human treasures than he can have some feathers.

III

Icarus starts stealing feathers wherever he can find them. When his father kills a wounded pelican, he sneaks the feathers inside his tattered shirt, and later takes his booty to the clock tower. He hangs the feathers by bits of dried sea-weed twine from the iron rafters. He loves to stand among them and let the breeze make the feathers, white, gray, blue, and brown, twirl and twist in the air. He imagines he's in a sea of wings, and as the feathers brush his face he fancies he can feel them merging into him, becoming his.

He draws mountains with charcoal, craggy peaks covered in trees, birds nesting, deer bedding down in grass. He's not sure if his dreams are right, but he needs a goal to work towards. Mountains are taller than skyscrapers, at least as far as he can understand. Surely there are some left, unleveled, thrusting above the water.

He studies the curvature of the feathers, the way one little piece interlocks with the other. He admires how the feathers are both hard and soft, yielding yet strong. He sketches the shape of feathers and wings on the floor of the clock tower with charcoal. He compares his sketches to the real counterparts hanging all around him. He rubs out his drawings and fixes the flaws. He also draws a ship with wings surrounded by suns. His father told him once that the sun is a star, and all of the stars are suns. At night sometimes he creeps to the window of the sky-scraper room they call home, and watches the night sky. He imagines being able to separate himself from water, from the atmosphere (which is apparently at least partly made out of water) and burst into the cool sharpness of space. He wonders if the stars make sounds like wings—a flock passing always overhead.

He starts observing the way wings work and he thinks that the shoulders of the bird, clenching and flexing, must look a lot like his father's shoulders when he rows. Icarus gathers even more feathers in secret. In the abandoned sky-scrapers he starts looking for large pieces of lightweight metal and wood, as well as tools. He finds a dead bird on a roof, and instead of telling his father or bringing it home to augment dinner, he takes the bird to the clock tower and furls and unfurls the bird's wings. He begins to work. Every day just as dawn begins to stain the night he sneaks away and works on his wings. He knows he can't really fly into space like his father, because of the lack of air up there, but he's fairly, nearly, certain he can join with the birds. His hands ache and his eyes feel heavy. He's not sleeping enough, and keeping a secret from his father is extremely difficult.

His father keeps shooting him strange glances and then shrugging, as though he lacks the energy to chase down his son's secrets. One day his father catches him staring out a window, eyes fixed on the sea. He grips his shoulders tightly, and Icarus flinches. He thinks his father's hands feel like the claws on a sea-gull.

"I don't want to be hard, you know," his father says. But he doesn't let go of Icarus's shoulders.

Icarus turns around and looks at his father, studies his thin cheeks, his reddened face, eyes in a permanent squint.

"I was just watching the sea."

"You were watching the birds," his father says.

"The sea-birds," Icarus says.

"Cheeky brat. Go catch some fish." His father ruffles his hair with his other hand and then releases his shoulders.

"There's nothing else to look at," Icarus says.

But his father doesn't answer. He's already gone, off to do some task, some preparation for a future that Icarus can't begin to understand. He wishes he knew where his father went, so that he could sneak off to the clock tower without discovery. He considers waiting. He sits, he stares out the window some more, he lies on his back and stares at the ceiling. He counts water spots for the hundredth time. Then he stands up and goes downstairs. He takes the littlest of the boats tied up against their skyscraper home and goes to his tower.

#

Back in the clock tower Icarus examines the bird he found, the one he skinned and let turn into a skeleton. He starts to make his own wing skeleton made out of scavenged metal and plastic, modeled after the bird. He sets them both on the floor and shapes one to mirror the other. His fingers bleed, but unlike when the gulls pecked him, he feels exhilarated. Even the sound of the waves feels less omnipresent than before he began his project. He starts to add feathers, stitching them to the frame, and every step of the way he tries the wings on, strapping them to his back.

Now, he stands at the edge of the clock tower and looks out at the water stretching over the edge of the horizon, at the birds owning the air. He flexes his shoulders. He's certain his wings, when they are finished, will flex with him. He holds out his arms. Soon, he says to the air, soon. He smiles. His father will be so proud. Surely he will. He thinks of his mother, studying plants, tending tender green leaves, of his father, up in space, looking for a new home. He doesn't believe that all of the mountains are leveled. He thinks all of the birds have to come from somewhere. They can't all be living off fish. He imagines his mother, who somehow is never dead in his mind. He thinks she might be on one of those mythical mountains, looking at the clouds, at the birds, just as he is him.

He hears footsteps in the tower. He turns, drops his arms, his phantom wings dropping to his sides. For a moment he imagines the footsteps belong to the mother he doesn't remember, or perhaps imagines. He remembers a gentle person who smells like the bar of white soap he found in a skyscraper once, clean and salt free, someone who will declare his wings fine workmanship. But as his father appears at the top of the stairs, he feels foolish for his dreams, and he smiles too brightly at his father.

"I've been studying," he says. He knows from the tattered books they've found that it's good for children to study.

His father stands, feet wide apart, scanning the room, the bird bones hanging from the ceiling, the feathers twirling from strings of kelp, the drawings on the floor—his father's eyes settle on the unfinished wings where Icarus so carefully placed them. He strides over to Icarus, grabs his hand, and holds it up to the light coming in from the window.

"You've made your fingers bleed," he says.

"I'm sorry," Icarus says.

His father drops his hand and goes over to the wings. He picks them up, turns them around. A gust of wind comes through the window and makes Icarus shiver and the wings quiver in his father's hands. Icarus doesn't know if he should tell his father to be careful or ask him to admire his workmanship.

Then his father tears the wings in half and throws them out the window. Icarus runs to the edge of the stone sill and stares, watches the wings fall apart, feathers captured by the wind, the frame heading inexorably toward the sea. Icarus hates the sea, hates how it eats everything, and hates its cold winds, its endless fish, and the dark unanswering wetness of its depths. He turns and looks at his father. He's clenching his fists at his side without noticing.

"I made those," he says.

His father scrubs across the charcoal drawings with his boot, smearing them, erasing them. Icarus drops to the stone floor, grabs his father's leg, pulls, tries to save one corner of the sketched wing, one piece of the skeletal system. His father shakes him off, lets him scramble on the floor. His father grabs the feathers, the bird skeleton, all of his makeshift tools, and throws them out the window too. He picks Icarus off the ground and pulls him back to the window, makes him watch his collection fall toward the water.

"That would have been you," his father says.

Icarus swallows the denial, the word no, the phrase *I don't believe you*. He starts to cry and then tries to stop crying. He spits the taste of salt out of his mouth. He can't stop his tears. His father lets go of him and kneels to look him in the eye.

"Don't ever do that again," he says.

Icarus looks away, and his father sighs, and stares out of the window.

"We used to fly, but it didn't do us any good. We still lost the entire world. Just be content, son."

Icarus swallows hard, trying not to cry, but his throat just hurts and tears come anyway.

"Mother wouldn't want me to give up," he says.

"She's dead, gone, under the sea, she can't want anything," his father says, totally without intonation.

Then he stands and walks down the stairs, his footsteps echoing. He doesn't look at Icarus, he doesn't mention Icarus's tears. Icarus wants to call him back, but he doesn't know what would happen, or what he would say, so he doesn't.

He looks at the charcoal remnants on the floor, at the tattered debris of his creation, pieces of feathers and very small bones, kelp unweighted by feathers and bones, now rioting from the rafters in the ever-present wind. He starts to pick up the pieces and wrap them carefully in his shirt, wondering where he can hide them from his father's gaze. His father forgot to smear the mountains scratched on the walls. Icarus stares at his drawing and hates the inadequacy of what he's made. He rubs his arm across his eyes, smearing his drying tears, and spits to get the taste of salt out of his mouth.

He imagines his wings slowly gliding into the deep, the pieces swirling in unseen currents, down and down, past the blind windows of the skyscrapers, past fish, all the way to the bottom. Perhaps they will find his mother, mingle with her bones. Perhaps his wings will land on one of the drowned spaceships, maybe the one his father flew. Perhaps they will rest with their cousins in aborted flight.

 MATT SCHUMACHER

INVISIBLE CITIES: NARRATIVE DERIVE AND THE RECOVERY OF SURREALIST MYSTERY

Italo Calvino's *Invisible Cities* frames its narrative as a dialogue between an authoritarian Tartar emperor, Kubla Khan, and an adventurous Venetian explorer, Marco Polo. The novel, then, may be seen to proceed through a dialogue between state-sanctioned rule and imagination. In his *Six Memos for the Next Millennium*, Calvino highly prizes "Visibility" as a vanishing value civilization should save: he indicts the modern "prefabricated image" as a threat to our ability to visualize, and to imagine. During Invisible Cities' dialogic exchanges between Polo and Khan, a rapport emphasized by both style and italics, Kubla questions, and Polo answers. When Khan accuses Polo of having never left the garden, or of having invented these cities, the tale becomes a metaphor for authorial imagination.

Such a metaphor seems apt: the cities themselves, a narrative of eccentric plans, unpredictable insistences, and obsessions built anew which is narratologically "torn down" and reconstructed again for the sake of each new tale, may be viewed as a way of eluding Kubla's rule. If some of these cities Polo speaks of are indeed imaginary, they exist as spaces in which Kubla cannot intervene. The cities seem largely dependent upon and part of the traveler, and incomplete until the traveler has fully experienced them; Armilla, for instance, is an unfinished nymph or naiad's network of pipes, and Zemrude, an urban space that fluctuates depending on "the mood of the beholder." Polo keeps moving in nomadic fashion from city to city, a transient narrator, or *homo ludens* the French situationists might be proud of; this nomadic style finds its correlative in the city of Eutropia, for example, which is many cities, shifting in its definition, based on the transience of its citizenry. As a nomad, Polo avoids the shadow of the law, and retains autonomy, is less subject to the scrutinizing eye and categorizing gaze of the emperor. Ultimately, these are Polo's cities, "cities of memory" and "cities of desire," spaces similar to those envisioned by the French surrealists and situationists, and this is his novel, more than it is Kubla's, although the latter occupies the throne.

Seldom do Khan's questions not endeavor to assess progress or the possible spoils of colonization. He represents his empire as a giant chessboard. Such squarish and functionalist cartography would please Haussman or Corbusier. "Shall I be able to possess my empire at last?" Khan asks his famous explorer. "The other ambassadors," Khan poses,

> "...warn me of famines. extortions.
> conspiracies, or else they inform me of newly discovered
> turquoise mines, advantageous prices in marten furs, sug-
> gestions for supplying damascened blades. And you?" the
> Great Khan asked Polo, "you return from lands equally
> distant and you can tell me only the thoughts that come to
> man who sits on his doorstep at evening to enjoy the cool
> air. What is the use, then, of all your traveling?"(27)

To venture an answer to the Great Khan's question, Polo's replies in these dialogues, and his replies enumerated in the cities he describes, are truly useful as case studies that open the mind to possibility. Their "cool air" diverts and fascinates the ruler, asking him to envision his kingdom as mysterious and complex, endlessly diverse, and cleverly systematic. Polo is able to distill the city for Kubla, but his distillation, rather than simplifying these cities, merely deepens their mystery, a mystery that, often, the surrealists would appreciate. In Hypatia, for example, a contemplation of magnolia gardens, blue lagoons, and beautiful bathing ladies transforms into a vision of the crabs eating the eyes of seaweed-haired suicides on the lagoon bottom. Through Polo's unique narrative imagination, Kubla is encouraged to see the empire in a less instrumental or numerical sense, to see his kingdom as a rich, diverse, elusive, and surprising space, to reconsider his kingdom as the utopian space it might be. While fanciful on the surface, and distinguished by their flights of imagination and urban eccentricity, Polo's replies disarm the kind of reductive generalities and efficiency that lead to war and greed. They focus the king on the particular. They revitalize Kubla's gratitude and kingly humility. To quote Polo, "the traveler recognizes the little that is his, discovering the much he has not had and will never have."

 ## STACEY BALKUN

APPLE-CHILD IN THE WOODS

She wanders up trunks to fall
from their limbs. She trusts

her bones to stay whole.
She grew from an apple seed
but no, its cyanide speck

didn't mark her flesh.
Her mother was an orchard

and a human mother, too,
who feasted on apple cores
and cassava root raw. Growing

in a root womb, she tasted
water and dirt, minerals sifting

into her wet flesh: she developed
a taste for poison. She's tough
as a pit in your teeth

and you can break skin,
dig to her core, but there—

her small self—a star
of venom in six acrid seeds.
Chew them and you'll burn.

John W. Sexton

THE FINEST

The doll came out of the ground, head first,
wedged between the prongs of the garden fork.
At first I took its head for a late turnip,
for turnips had been set in this patch earlier.
But the doll opened one eye
and I saw it then for what it was.
I pulled the fork gently
and the rest of the doll surfaced,
a ragged floral dress left hanging on its body.

The doll's other eye remaining closed,
I washed its stiff body under the garden tap.
Still the colour of mud, the doll recovered just enough
for a whirring to erupt in its throat,
and out came a single word, "Dada."
Her hair was muddy-coloured too, but looked just right.
In fact, mud seemed her natural colour.

In the kitchen I propped the doll on the table.
The whirring erupted again.
"Why did you leave me, Dada?"
"I didn't leave you," I said;
"I found you while I was turning the ground
for a late sowing of cabbage. I am not your Dada,
but I will be your Dada if you like."

I went to prepare some tea.
When I returned, the doll was wearing
a new poncho dress, roughly cut at the neck

from a folded checked tea-towel, but with no need of sewing.
My nail scissors lay on the table.
To cover her feet she had made slippers by cutting two fingers
from a pair of my gloves.
"Tomorrow I will buy you new clothes," I said.

"Tomorrow, Dada, you will dig us back into the ground;
and we will be dressed forever, in the finest of deaths.
We will never be lost again, because death never dies."
Then she opened her other eye for the first time
and held my gaze.

Study for Deadfall

 MIRANDA SCHMIDT

FAMILIAR

He was never the same from one day to the next, by which I mean he was never quite shaped the same way. Some days he was small, some days large. Some days he was furry and some days he wasn't. Some days he had sharp teeth and some days he had no teeth at all.

His wife never knows, each morning, what shape she will wake up beside. She only knows that it will be a different shape from the one that she fell asleep next to.

Sometimes he repeats shapes, but never two days in a row. Sometimes a week or two or three will go by and she'll recognize the same shape again. The recognition always makes her happy—the relieved kind of happy, not the ecstatic kind—because it makes her believe that there might be a limited number of shapes that her husband can turn into, that, one day, she might recognize all of them so that every iteration will become familiar.

I don't know very much about this woman. I don't know if she is rich or poor, if she considers herself plain or beautiful. She is, I know, a wife but she is not, I think, a mother, though one day she might be. She has a mother somewhere and a father too, I suppose. I don't know where, though. I don't know who. She may or may not have siblings. She must have friends somewhere, but I don't think she sees them often anymore, not since her husband began changing shape, which was quite some time ago but not so long ago that she has forgotten what it was to be married to someone singular, to someone whose consistent man-shape gave at least the illusion of solidity.

No, she does not see many people these days. She goes to work and she comes home and her colleagues think she is quiet and reserved and responsible, a classic introvert. She does not know, any longer, how to talk about herself, cannot find the words to describe the life she is now living. There is no language, she thinks, to tell of this thing that is happening, of a human/man/husband turned bear/turned rodent/turned fish/ snake/bird/lizard. There is no way to describe it that does not seem laughable or fable-ish. And it feels neither laughable nor fable-ish—except when it does, except when the absurdity of her husband turned mouse hits her and she smiles and can't help but pick him up and put him in her pocket and take him with her to work, sneaking him cheese from her sandwich at lunch and reaching her hand inside to stroke his tiny soft head, his thumbeline ears, his quivering tail.

Sometimes, though, it is merely frustrating. When, for instance, he gnawed through the couch cushions, his wild canine teeth sunk deep in their stuffing as he growled and drooled and shook his way through. Or when he kicked the door down and splintered the cupboards with his strong elk legs.

And, sometimes, it is frightening, like the time he turned tiger and spent the morning eyeing her in hungry predation until, unnerved, she backed her way into the bathroom, locking the door behind her. She slept in the bathtub that night, listening to him pacing the hallway outside the door. She knows he will never hurt her, knows he loves her, knows he feels this whatever shape he is in, but sometimes, on days like the tiger day, she begins to have doubts.

Sometimes, on the days he turns human again, it is sad. It didn't use to be. He used to speak to her on those days, describe what it felt like to be shaped like a fox or a salamander or a crow. She used to look forward to those days when they could talk again, compare their experiences of his transformations.

"You were so cute," she'd tell him, "As that golden retriever. So darling."

"I could smell everything," he'd say, eyes wide with the wonder of it, "It was so *exciting*."

But now, he hardly speaks at all. Now, his eyes look weary and distant, as if, even person-shaped, he is no longer entirely human, no longer entirely hers. She wonders, now, on those days, as she watches him lie on the couch staring up at the ceiling, whose he is if not hers, what he is if not human.

And, as I watch her watch him, I wonder about the skins we exist in, the words we are kept in, the stories that form and reform us, that are formed and reformed by us, that hold us together and that hold us apart. I wonder, if she tried, if this woman could change with her husband or if that sort of change is impossible. I wonder if that question is fair. I wonder if she knew in some way, when she married the human-shaped man, if she could sense, even then, some kind of shifting just under his surface. I wonder if that's a part of why she loved him in the first place, that metamorphic nature, that hint of uncertainty within.

She doesn't, though, wonder this. She doesn't think of whys or hows. She is beyond whys and hows now. She is securely locked into the what. What shape will he be? What will he do? What will I do? What will we be like?

Jonathan Louis Duckworth

FOLKLORE

Noun.
(Tales,
legends, beliefs of a certain people.)

                We hide our hearts
in carved wooden eggs,
in the bellies of hollow trees,
beneath tangles of roots,
& pray we won't lose our
keys & maps & direction.

The old ghost dangles from a branch
by the trail of her moonwhite hair. She
expects no rescue;
                waits for night to muffle
                the world;
that she can disappear with dignity.

In the cold house of piled stone,
the Black Miller grinds the cosmos
down to nothing, one small
piece at a time.
                On this swept path
through the deep weald, you walk
in mincing steps. Somewhere ahead
your carcass & your own unblinking
eyes wait for you to catch up.

We build our folklore like mazes
                    only because
the naked truth of our world
has spines too long, too sharp,
& must be padded in the fur
of a dark wolf; in the mothgnawn
kirtle of a witch who spins gold
from the cilia of our throats.
& the story we keep telling is that

"This is all just a story."

 STEVE CASTRO

TWO POEMS

A DEADLY CURSE

She opened wide, inviting me to enter her mouth.
She looked like Buddha.

"No, thank you," I replied.

She shut her trap. An Andean condor perched on her left shoulder.

She yawned and as she did so, the condor flew into her open mouth.
The Buddha closed her mouth, then began sewing her lips shut.

We were facing each other ten feet apart. I was kneeling on the ground.
She was floating two feet in the air with her legs crossed
in a sitting position. I got up, turned around and walked away.

I then looked back and saw condor wings
growing out of the Buddha's back.

"May the sky swallow you whole," I told her.

Her lips were sewn shut, so she didn't reply.

FIRE PROOF

By definition, a watch is a time machine.

The perfect machine is made of flesh.

A bird with a mechanical soul was entrapped
inside a cuckoo clock, which was cursed.
That clock burned down, along with the abode
That housed it. After the mansion burned to the ground,
a van pulled up on the premises. Three men
from the future searched through the ashes.
They were looking for a bird with a mechanical soul,
which was in fact, the world's first time machine.

 Andrew Dobbs

THE OTHER SIDE

There is a road, and on one side of this road is a chicken. On the other side, the grass is greener. You are the chicken, and the chicken is you.

The road is a one-lane dirt road. When you try to cross it, you are incinerated by a nuclear bomb. In that brief-but-eternal instant before you die, you wonder why anyone would drop a nuke on a chicken.

#

This is chicken heaven: In front of you is a road, and on the other side, the grass is greener. Before you decide to cross it, you wonder whether heaven has nuclear warfare, or any other sort of warfare, or bombs at all. Probably not, but they might have cars, so you decide to find a crosswalk.

Sometime after crossing the crosswalk and before the end of your story, you meet the Great Chicken God, who is both great and godly.

"So," you ask the Great Chicken God, "which came first ... the chicken or the chicken god?"

#

This is chicken hell: In front of you is a road; you call a cab. The cabby is a chicken with its head chopped off. The head dangles from the rearview mirror, attached by a rope. Its beady eyes watch the road while the head rocks back and forth.

"Is it just me," you ask the cabby, "or is the grass greener on that side of the road, as compared to this side?"

The head swivels around, gaping at you in silence.

You stare at the head as it turns back to watch the road. You gaze out the window.

#

This is the other side: The grass is definitely greener.

Sometime after finding the greener grass, and before the end of your story, you meet a worm.

"Who are you?" the worm asks.

"A chicken," you say, slightly perturbed as you scratch the ground. You peck--

The worm wriggles away. "Must you do that?"

"Habit," you say.

"It's rather disturbing to me," the worm says, "if you don't mind my saying."

"I only eat chicken feed," you say.

"All the same."

"Alright, alright," you say. "What's your name anyhow?"

"Wirgil."

"Wirgil?"

"Just call me Willy." He wriggles. "It's time to go."

"Go where?"

#

This is human heaven: There are lots of bright, white lights. In front of you is a road. It is made of gold.

"Let's cross it," you suggest to Willy.

Sometime after crossing the gold road and before the end of your story, you meet some angels standing by some pearly gates. Before you can say anything stupid about the proximity of said angels to said arch-like gates, Willy the worm pulls you through to a number dispenser.

"Take a number," he explains.

Sometime later (the exact time being dependent on your number, the time taken between each number, and whether or not you're bored), your number is called.

You approach a counter and hand the number to the ticket taker.

"And where do you want to go?" he asks.

"Heaven, please," Willy says.

"Take that escalator over there."

"That's it?" you ask.

"I'm just the ticket guy." He shrugs. "Ever since heaven became a democracy, all I do is take your ticket and point you in the right direction."

"A democracy?" you ask. "What's that?"

"It's better," the Ticket Guy says.

"Better than what?"

"Communism."

"Isn't there anything else?" Willy asks.

"We used to be a monarchy," he says.

"So what does God do now?" Willy asks.

"You must mean Jesus." The Ticket Guy nods. "He's the President."

"Actually, I think I mean someone else," Willy says. "The Great Human God."

"We don't have one," he says.

"You don't have one?" you ask.

"We did, but He died."

"Died?" Willy asks.

"Pneumonia."

"Pneumonia? That's absurd!" Willy wriggles (slightly perturbed).

"Yes." The Ticket Guy shrugs again. "God is dead. Supposedly, at least. I mean, no one knows of course. The only ones who've ever seen him are Jesus and a couple prophets. But as far as it goes for the rest of us, I haven't seen him myself, so I don't know, you know?"

"I don't get it," you say.

The Ticket Guy looks around and leans closer. "Well, just know that I'm not saying I don't know." He points to an escalator. "You better go ride that escalator before heaven's not a democracy anymore."

#

This is the escalator to heaven:

"What's that warning sign for?" you ask.

Willy squints at the sign. "It says, *Warning: In case of fire, first check to make sure you are not in hell. If you are not in hell, quit your bitching.*"

#

Somewhere in heaven, sometime after leaving the escalator and buying fish and chips from a carnie:

"What now?" you ask, plucking crumbs out of your feathers.

"We find Jesus," Willy says.

"Every other heaven I've been to, the Great God was just right there," you say, perturbed ever-so-slightly.

"Yes, but that wasn't human heaven. You can't just barge in on the President and ask a bunch of stupid questions."

"Then what do we do?"

#

This is a press conference: In front of you are the backs of reporters, and somewhere in front of them is the President.

"First, I would like to start off," Jesus begins, "before addressing other issues, the recent bad press about my administration regarding...well, we all know what it's regarding. Anyway, to get to my point, what I want to say is that there are things we know we are working on, and there are things we know we are not working on. But more than that, there are many things we do not know we are not working on, and many other things we do not know we are not-not working on...so quit your bitching. Any questions?"

"I have a question," you shout. "Which came first...the Great Human God or the President?"

"If by Great Human God," Jesus says, "you mean Dad, then yes, He came first, of course. But as we all know, He tragically died of pneumonia shortly before I became President. What's your point?"

"I never said I have one!"

"I have a question, too," Willy yells, perhaps a little too loudly, as the room is quite small. "If it's true that God died of pneumonia; if it's true that you're Jesus Christ and you've saved everyone from their sins; if this is really human heaven, the place where humans can go when they die; if the human Bible has all the knowledge anyone ever needs; if it's all true; if it's not all a figment of my imagination, then why the hell is the slogan of your administration 'quit your bitching'?"

#

Jesus' office: It is vaguely shaped like an egg, but then again, anything that's round looks like an egg to you.

"I don't see why your messenger called this a friendly little powwow," Willy says. "You obviously mean to give us the boot."

"Actually, I can't," Jesus says. "Unfortunately, it's still a democracy. Freedom. Life, Liberty, and the Pursuit of Etcetera. Would you please sit down?"

"Why?" Willy asks.

"I want to tell you a story."

You sit down. "A parable?"

"More or less," Jesus says. He sucks in a deep breath and begins. "A man walks into a bar. At a table, he sees a chicken, a worm, and me playing cards. So he asks the bartender, "Is that chicken playing cards?" and the bartender says, "Yes." Then he asks. "Is that worm playing cards?" and the bartender says, "Yes." Finally, he asks, "Is that Jesus playing cards?" and this time I answer, "I am the Way, the Truth, and the Life. No one comes to the Father but through me."

You scrape at the floor a few times, ruffle your feathers, and resist the urge to peck.

"That's it?" Willy ponders aloud.

"Go fish," Jesus answers.

#

This is human hell: There are an infinite number of roads around you, an asphalt web flickering in and out of existence. Willy is gone, and you are trying to find him. You can make out some greener grass here and there, but you don't know which road to cross.

Sometime after pecking at the ground perturbedly and before your story ends, you meet a giant desert tortoise.

"What are you doing here?" you ask the tortoise.

"Deus ex machina."

"What?"

"I'm the author," I say.

You ponder this for a moment and decide to ask something pertinent while you have the chance: "Am I going to find Willy?"

"More or less," I reply.

My response is not very satisfying. "What's that mean?" you ask. "Where did Willy go? Which road should I cross?"

"Don't know," I reply. I turn away from you and amble off. I look back. "The question is why."

#

This will be the future: You will find Willy again after twenty years. You will run into him, by chance, and this is what you will say:

"Willy?" You will be surprised at seeing him, and curious. "How are you?" you will ask.

He will seem unresponsive: "Fair enough."

The uncomfortable silence will bother you more than him. You will ruffle your feathers. "What have you been up to?"

"I've got to go." Willy will glance at his watch. "Going to be late."

"Right," you will say. "Well . . . good seeing you."

"So long," he will say, and then he will leave.

#

Sometime after this conversation and before you're dead, you will think of the things you didn't tell him. You will wonder why he left and what happened. You might question whether memories can sustain, if they can keep you alive.

Ten years later you will see him again. This time you will have a cup of coffee and thirty minutes to make up for thirty years. Most of it will be silence, and then he will tell you at the end:

"I'm ready to die."

"What happened?" you will ask.

"Nothing worked out."

He will stare into his cup of coffee, and you will sip yours.

"I saw you in hell with the tortoise," he will say.

"You did?"

"Back when you were still looking for me." He will pause. "I pretended I didn't see you, and then I hid."

"Why?"

"I don't know." He will glance at his watch. "I've got to go again. I'm sorry."

"It's okay," you will say. "At least we got half an hour, right?"

He will wriggle away. "See you later."

You will say goodbye to Willy, and then you will walk outside. In front of you will be a road and the end of your story. You might see, across the road, the green-green grass, and you might take a step, take a step, take a step...until you reach the other side.

 SETH JANI

NAVIGATORS

The spyglass opens over
The backwards treading sea
Where the shipwrecked travel
In reverse, entering the kingdom
On a boat of silver glass.
Their journey is just beginning,
The coral washed from their bodies
And a small charm of navigation
Hidden in their pockets.
They are pieces of star that fell
Like insect wings on the almost-
Drafted map. The one that shows
A continent to be discovered,
A red dragon at the very center.
Those flame-dark hills are only
Part of the imaginarium.
Just like the moon, stunning
The subtropic eye, with its
Dazzling road.

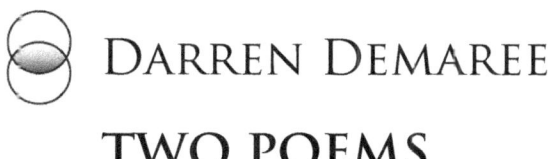 DARREN DEMAREE

TWO POEMS

YOU DON'T HAVE TO DIE WELL FOR ME #37

Thirty-seven minutes late & I have swirled all of the olive oil into an empty coffee can & I have rolled my wrist to collect all of the remaining grains in the thick yellow sea & I have done this without finding the metaphor. If my parents entered my house right now, they would enter from different doors & each of them would ask me if I was lost. The children think I can do magic. None of my neighbors have ever knocked on our door. I believe enough in witchcraft to know not to call what I'm doing witchcraft.

YOU DON'T HAVE TO DIE WELL FOR ME #39

Thirty-nine minutes late & I have lost the pulse of where my dreams come from, I have lost your incidents completely, I have traveled a new order of my own psyche & I have swam while standing up on the hardwood floors of our living room. I have put on & taken off a hat dozens of times. I was, for ten seconds, my own father & I took that opportunity to never forgive myself for turning this dial until it snapped off. I shouted those words into a whisper & lightning that came with my breath removed that anger & left me with your absence. I would have preferred to stay my father for much longer.

 ROSE SERVIS

TEST DAY

I wake up excited—it's test day. I kick off the covers and jump to the floor. My shoes are by the door, and I slip into them—grab my red coat—

A great fog slows us down on the way to school. We walk in clumsy twos and threes, our elbows linked and jaws rattling from the cold. The sky above is brilliant white static. It grows silvered around the edges. Walking into it, our skin feel creamy and touched. Thinking of the test, we chatter brightly about future celebrations, our crazy-beloved teachers. The group walking behind us lightly clips our heels. 'Sorry! Sorry!' Giddy shouts and giggles and all our hearts quicken, the collective stride lengthens—Now I am squinting to make out what is red close ahead. Looks like illuminated roses, but it is just three coats, more of our own—

We duck into a bodega that sells egg and cheese sandwiches in the morning. While our breakfast cooks on the hotplate, we prowl the aisles. Our teacher is hunched at a little card table by the freezer. 'What! Drunk again!' we cry and begin prodding his shoulders with long fingers of shrink-wrapped jerky. An eye turns up to look at us, bloodshot and weeping crusts. We laugh, cheering, 'It's test day! Get up!' The eye closes. Our teacher mutters, 'I don't know you. Go away!' But we haul him up by the armpits, drag him outdoors—

We have no shadows but our breath pours out like little doubled bodies. What is Teacher doing now? Hacking up something hot and yellow. 'Old drunk,' the others hiss. I grow frightened—voices are rising. I see bright eyes. 'Quick!' I cry and reach for Teacher's arm, but snatch only vapors. He is already running.

I follow. Drumming footfalls on all sides—my competitors? But I see only the brown smudge of my teacher's coat up ahead. I call out, a breathless 'Wait!' But the silver fog spirals and twists. I lose sight of him.

I slow to a stop. Sweat leaks out of my skin, and panic creeps in. Until now, the fog has merely nipped and gnawed my fingertips, but now I feel it creep up my coat sleeves and slip down my collar to my quivering belly. I try to blink it back, but the fog is filling up my eyes. I see bright haze, even now that I've shut them.

Suddenly, in a burst of heat, he is at my side. Gin fumes startle my nostrils as he asks me, 'Ready to begin?'

I nod, then realize he can't see me. The fog is so thick that my right hand, flapping before my eyes, is gone. My eyes cross, but I can't see my nose. I open my mouth to give consent, but before I can say a word, I feel the first item drop into my palm.

It is altogether little. A shallow hole.

With a grin, I declare, 'THIMBLE!'

A second object replaces the first. *This could be dark and light.* I think of *ribbon, machinery, charm.*

'HANDKERCHIEF!' I cry.

The second item is gone, while a third dribbles down. *Disappointing,* I determine. *But unlikely pus.*

'WAX!'

And on and on. My teacher, standing mute and invisible beside me in the impenetrable fog, places objects in my hand. With my inner senses, my inner eye and inner touch, I isolate their essential characteristics to identify what they are.

Simple little middles— 'BUTTONS!'

Solid, frantic. Makes dark chasm— 'PEN!'

The identifications increase in difficulty. I am sweating despite the cold, soon shouting, BLACK, CLIMATE, METHOD, RELEASE, CHOKE, WAIST, THAT, FRIGHTFUL, MALACHITE.

Another item is placed for my determination. It lies lightly. I hesitate. *Supposing beautiful use. Sight, more shining. All surrounding fine complication.*

'DRAWING!' I say, and here is a new one, weighing heavily. *No, not sister. One mismanaged. Only animosity shows.* 'CAT!' I cry and it is replaced by *slim crackle, elbow shadow. This is why less.* 'DUST!' I determine and am correct and am feeling now *soldier white slender, all tassel, nearly wrist, it's—*

'GLITTER?'

Hesitation has crept into my voice. *Rising intonation, telltale defeat.* I hear it as it happens, and my heart falls. I have misidentified the object. I am finished. A failure! While my companions march onward toward bright futures, I will crawl back into the dark bedrooms of my parents' home.

The misidentified object is taken from me. I hold my breath, awaiting correction, my final grade.

But it doesn't come. Instead of *my* determination, I am given a new object. *Not white, not really thing—*it's obvious what it is, but I say nothing. *Why didn't Teacher correct me?*

Doesn't he know I got it wrong? A budding tightness in my chest, a terrible suspicion.

Who is this testing me? Is this really Teacher?

The object slips through my fingers, into the fog. I am reaching out into gray-blue vapors, still too thick to see through, despite a temperature change, a perceptible warming. As I wave my hands in the loose air, I strike a burlap coat. I grab it and pull it toward me, my hands spidering up the sandy fabric to the moist dough of Teacher's face.

My fingers grope his features. I grow increasingly dismayed—

'What, tiny ears?'

'What, tiny eyes?'

'What, tiny mouth?'

'What, tiny head?'

I snatch my hands back. I step away. 'Who are you?' I cry.

All around I see red coats gathering. The fog is dispersing, revealing pairs and pairs of roses in gloom. Teacher, imposter-teacher, is trembling in the center of our bloody circle. Our memory seizes upon what he himself has taught us, an old German tune. In unison, we sing—

Strip his clothes off, then he'll teach us!

If he doesn't, kill him dead!

Only a teacher, only a teacher

He stumbles back, gasping—

'No, no! But who were you expecting?'

Not you. Someone better, greater, like we will be. And we approach him.

 REBECCA LILLY

THREE POEMS

FOREST MINIATURES

Silence unstitches the mind from tapestries of dream: the dew-heavy cobwebs bridging rocks, branches and leaves, trapping moths and other insects to be eaten.

A sorcerer scuffles through cobwebs, stopping by my window at dusk. *"The heart is a crystal needing polish. Your memories are rocks on the river bottom, the deepest buried in red mud."*

"I care little for what's buried," I confessed, pointing up (the sun almost gone; moon, barely a glow over the mountain). *"I'd rather find crystals of rainfall from cumulus."*

"—stone-faced clouds which mirror who we are won't let us glimpse the stars," the seer interrupted. I'd left my window open; the forest was dark. I peered out; he was right. Not one star.

"Ah, well," I shrugged, closing the window screen, *"I never rely on the night when no stars are visible, but on daylight, when sun breaks through the clouds and canopies."*

"Our sun is just one *star,"* the sorcerer re-plied, annoyed at my complaisance, *"and certainly not the brightest."* Frowning, he left my cottage for the forest and returned at dawn, knocking at my door.

"Oblige me, and I'll show you the tapestry of stars," he offered, pointing to a boulder in the woods. I watched from my cottage as fog lifted from leaves of lower branches and tufts of grass—while he sat the whole morning threading weaves of lichen and mosses in the boulder clefts.

When sun struck the droplets, the green weave sparkled, as did the cobwebs full of curled leaves, sagging with flies and moths. Even with the power of spells, the sorcerer isn't a deity: he can't *bring into being,* only offer us a sense of what's missing.

BLOODROOT

1.

In *The Book of Life and Death* are proofs for soul's existence, but references are infinite and therefore of no help. Each of us constructs an endpoint from abstractions and epiphenomena.

The epigraph reads:

"Truth can be intuited from questions alone—it must be when the conclusion's paralogical.

The *Book* has several volumes and authors (mostly anonymous) who offer lengthy footnotes:

"...insofar as the body is a blood root, water seeks its own level, the point of least resistance from which to evolve. Water crystallizes, yet sunlight inhabits the cells' virtual particles, flashing in spirals, radiating out in infinitesimals."

2.

I close the book, falling back into myself under a pine in a wildflower field. I imagine others in the past who held the book, questioning the lapse of a familiar self.

Bloodroot in the field is the first sign of spring. Resembling a daisy—white petals, yellow centers—it closes in evening. It has a single irregular leaf; and an orange sap, the "blood" in its stem. As I think of it, I'm losing its image and its essence, left with shadowy thoughts of the underground stem sprouting wings from milky sap.

Closing my eyes, I rest my back against the pine trunk; the moment drags with remembered abstraction. From a petal, a dust speck flashes—a phoenix winging down to detritus and ash—passed over as a firefly dying on the field path.

THE VIRTUAL FLOWER FIELDS

Lucifer fingered the sleeves of his black velvet suit and scarlet tie as he leaned across the cemetery fence. "The dead are full of lies and regrets. I'm not the least interested in your enticements," I said.

"Your malaise is called the *twilight effect*. In the virtual flower fields" (with a white spidery hand, he gestured past the fence) "is a country with all manner of elixirs, fields of butterfly weed and blackberry lily!" He was a terrible salesman for the other side and I despised his hackneyed attempts.

"Naturally," I said, "each of us wants a genie who grants wishes at will. Our affairs of business require us to travel but the wisest need no path and regard sightseeing as a distraction."

Lucifer smiled, undeterred in his attempts to sell otherworldly journeys, as if he had a travel brochure. His black fingernails belied him, flashing and gesturing toward half-lit clouds.

Beyond the fence was rubble and rough paths to the mountains, foothills winding down to the sea. I recalled the sorcerer's warning when he'd bequeathed me the cemetery: *The soul throughout its journey is a foundling, never reconciled to its history, or to its footprints in the virtual flower fields, spellbound by destiny.*

Tree Storm Dance

D. LEWIS

SOMETHING LIKE A HAUNTING

And the county executive, whenever he felt like this, had trouble breathing, he simply could not get air, felt like he was already too full, like there was no room for anything else inside him besides what was already inside him, and, no matter how much air he gulped (so much air he practically choked on it), his body still told him it was drowning, he was suffocating, expiring in his very own personal vacuum, each cell in his body crying out for a type of oxygen he couldn't quite possibly seem to give it; and it was this kind of molecular, subatomic, quantum-level breathlessness (which was closely related to the county executive's overfullness, his illogical overfullness, paradoxical even: an overfullness of stuff that felt like nothing at all) that kept the county executive awake at night, lying in bed, pillow punching his face, sheets laughing between his legs, boxers performing a function primarily absorbent in nature; and the county executive, wide awake, tossing, turning, tormented by the proximity of sleep, the nearness of escape, its promise, while wrestling with the silent injunction to endure, to just hold still, just a little while longer, don't move, count to ten, breathe—and feeling the whole time like he's positively bulging with overfullness, excrescent with it, misshapen by it in a way that makes lying in bed indescribably hellish: the county executive tossed and turned but always seeming to land squarely on it, this bulge, his overfullness, and wanted to scream it out, cry it out, vomit it out, purge, but, lacking any belief in cures (too afraid, at this point, even to risk hope), and also not wanting to disturb the body of his wife sleeping next to him, performing a nasal symphony there, her body a soft stillness, a countervailing force, center of gravity, something to orbit—the county executive instead simply lay awake, sleepless, watching the clock, partially visible to him in polygonal slats of canted moonlight, 1:14, the ticking of the second hand getting lost beneath the air conditioner clicking on, its distant hum, reassuring somehow, the inside of the house's insides revealing their very own proper functioning, 1:27, the glass of water on the nightstand within reach without rolling over, beaded condensation trickling down, pooling on the woodgrain's dark finish, evaporating imperceptibly, and 1:53, the urge to pee, and 2:16, time passing like that, and 3:04, with nothing to do, nothing to be done, nowhere to go, no action to be taken, no difference to be made, 3:12, and now everything the county executive could possibly think of—

everything: both waking and sleeping, stirring and keeping still, breathing and not breathing, i.e., every conceivable direction in which the county executive's agency could possibly be expressed—appeared to him now as less an escape from than an expression of his breathless overfullness, and 3:35, masturbation not an option, the overfullness not expressive in that way, testicles not a thought suppressor, prostate little more than a buckle cavity, penis exhaling into downward-facing dog, the whole of his sexual being reduced to little more than a rhetorical question, and 5:38, getting up, rising as if automatically, feeling no more rested, no less breathlessly overfull than the night before, but having lost all interest in even the appearance of sleep, and now resigned to meeting the day with a solemn nod, an act of recognition, a heartfelt ugh, the county executive proceeded to enter the master bathroom to spend, as he did every morning, his first few waking moments in front of the mirror, working to erase all evidence of the previous night's sleeplessness, the drawn-and-quartered expression it left his face in—the county executive gently massaged his eyes and cheeks and temples, the corners of his mouth; pinched the bridge of his nose, squinting, trying to mold his features back into human form; and, having done this— having done this then disrobed and showered, having toweled dry and re-robed and gone downstairs for breakfast, having found his wife already there, in the kitchen, where she greeted him with a cheerful "Good Morning!," the cheer of which sounded slightly forced—the county executive's features, the second he forgot them, reverted back to their resting state: the distant and vacantly pained expression of a person through whom an invisible electrical current is running every second of every day without interruption (nor so much as even a hint of ever really truly stopping), and, sitting down now at the kitchen table, his face having already slipped away from him, the county executive began to feel (as he would for the rest of the day) reduced by his overfullness to a tiny speck inside himself, excluded by it from the physical space his body occupied—actually physically displaced by the overfullness that had consumed him—it was like the county executive was actually six inches to the left of wherever he appeared to others to actually, physically be, such that their gaze never met his nor his theirs; such that whatever was said to him flew right past his ear, never so much as even nicking its flesh, rendering him lobeless; such that whenever anyone reached out to touch him, they missed and were forced to simply assume that he, the county executive, had recoiled perhaps even faster than they'd reached out to touch him, which assumption they—the county executive's wife and son, his friends and colleagues—wore on their faces like billboards of concern, and, upon seeing this from his sidelong vantage point six inches to the left of wherever he actually appeared to be, the county executive felt the urge to apologize, but the things—what were they called?—he was supposed to use to make the thing he felt compelled to make, an apology (which wasn't a thing he was sure he could actually make, even if he could remember the things he was supposed to make it out of, or at least what the latter things were called)—the county executive wasn't particularly confident he could force them out from between his lips: his voice box having long ago been reduced to a saliva generator, his tongue now a kind of sponge, and the place the apology was supposed to come from, the ache machine, having been consumed totally by the very same overfull condition that caused the physical dislocation he felt an urgent need to apologize for, such that the county executive felt helpless, truly helpless, to communicate his sincere wish to apologize to any one of the now literally almost innumerable people he felt a very real and sincere wish to apologize to; and, now, considering this as he sat down at the kitchen table in his home's breakfast nook, facing the wall, his wife and son circulating throughout the house around him, the county executive tried and failed to put food in his food hole (his condition of being six inches to the left of wherever he actually appeared to be causing him no end of difficulty in this regard: his mouth always six inches to the right of where he felt it should be; his fork hand always six inches to the left of where it looked like it was, and the operation of making the two meet at some conjectural point in between requiring more concentration than he had to spare (again, due to the overfullness's constant distraction, which made focusing on anything outside it, over and above it, beyond it, etc., for more than a second or two at a time, virtually impossible for the county executive, but which— the overfullness, not the distraction—at least kept the county executive from feeling all that hungry as he watched first eggs, then bacon, then two pieces of dry, whole wheat toast fall to his feet then the floor

# SARAH KAIN GUTOWSKI

TWO POEMS

LIGHTNING
(Transfiguration and Punishment)

I.

Once the children left the meadow, their ghosts hanging
  like clouds of dust and fog that couldn't burn away
  in the wet air, the woman's panic thickened, too,
  as if it were layers of sky descended, blanketing
  her skin and stopping her mouth and nose until breathing
  became a chore, a ragged labor, and then it crawled
  to fits and starts, full stops followed by deep inhalations.
  The sparrow's carcass slid from her open palm to the ground.
When the dust began to crawl with ants, she staggered back to her tower.

The hearth was filled with glowing ash, its smoldering light
  the only moving part of the room. Inside her chamber
  the air was slick with cold and dew, its surfaces
  collecting water beads and the sheen of saturation.
  The knife she'd used to free her heart, that distressed bird,
  lay among the cogs and wheels from the shattered clocks,
  the fine blade dull with blood. She picked it up, and pain,
  its phantom, flashed inside her chest like sudden applause.
She opened her mouth and raised the knife. Then she cut her tongue off.

Her mouth, hot with its fresh wound, filled with dark liquid.
  Its overflow spilled to the floor, a wash that pooled and gleamed

more red in the weak light of the room. She threw her tongue,
uncurled and limp, onto the ash and piled wood
on top, hiding its monstrous length. She lit the tinder.
Slow as sunrise, flames began to rise. Light broke
across the marble floor and onto the woman's face.
She thrust the knife into the blaze so it burned clean;
then she raised its blade to the stump and seared the flesh. Her wound was sealed.

She found again the silk, and the needle made of stone,
and through the open pocks along her lips she sewed
again the stitches, even though her mouth was emptied
of all threat. Blood that smeared her teeth clung to the threads,
staining them pink. The face she saw in the mirror looked
like she'd been painted wrong: a blur instead of a mouth,
her pupils lost within their dark brown irises,
her hair matted with dust and laced with twigs. At length,
she cleaned the tower floor, and then herself, and then she slept.

After fitful dreams she rose to a fitful world.
She watched the sun regain the sky, its cold gray light
tearing the shadowy trees to ribbons, whips of branches
that lashed back, raking clouds, refusing the sky its tether.
Something pulled at her as well. Small spheres of tangled
leaves tumbled across the brittle, brown lawn
and broke apart in the woods, catching in brambles that shook
as if they feared being crushed by the world overhead,
but she ignored the warning. Down the tower steps she fled

and into the building storm, its argument loud in her ears,
its anger deafening, its sudden, vain tears
washing her face as she walked between the trees and brush.
The field, where just the day before she'd scared the children,
moved its many hands in protest, the grass bent
away from her footsteps, every blade loathing her touch.

Against the wind she walked, pushed back by its solid arm,
  while thunder shook the air and lightning pared the sky.
A white bolt needled through her body into the ground, and she died.

II.

Two seasons passed. When the children began to feel safe,
  emboldened by sunshine, green leaves budding and birds returned,
  they found her remains: a batch of bones regurgitated
  by some monstrous owl, or dragon, a mess they barely knew
  as human, let alone belonging to *her*, the woman who'd once
  woven them gifts and kept them company in silence.
  Her dress was just a rag melted into the earth.
  The boy kicked loose a bone from the overgrown grass that choked
with her debris, and he held it aloft, as if he'd conquered a foe.

His sister remained more solemn, frightened by the ants
  that streamed in long black tears from the skull's empty stare,
  its teeth forever locked in the same disturbing smile.
  While her brother vanquished monsters with his femur-sword,
  she hurried back and forth between the creek and the bones,
  shuttling cups and saucers full of earth and rocks
  to cover the skull's unbearable grin. The little grave
  rose above the grass, a marker and reminder –
but they forgot about her, as children do, over time.

WHAT OUR MOTHERS WON'T NAME

How much wisdom has this shifting brought her?
At dawn, or at sun down, or high noon or midnight,
she is still the same dumb creature,
silent with her lack of correctness, the right language,
smart enough to recognize where she has failed
to enact the lessons of experience, despite their magic.
What use is transformation if it sits unused
in the atlas of the brain, growing outdated
as the world it represents breaks and reforms
again and again, with a purpose she senses
but cannot comprehend, beyond recognition?

The sow retreats into prostrate sulks
and the cramp of sleep, for what else can she feel
when she catches her reflection in the trough,
after seeing so many ways to live
in the world, and yet always returning
to the same, mute immovable bulk,
the same creature who will be acted upon,
and consumed, and consumed, and finally consumed?

There was always a hole in the fence
or sudden wings, strange but workable
extending from her spine, and an expanse of sky
or a sheltering forest waving its many invitations;
she could have left and yet she stayed,
she could have morphed but she remains
essentially unchanged, tongue thick in her mouth,
legs bent, her weight fixed to this spot,
this dent in the earth, this corner of air
in the stagnant yard, where she lies
while the flies build their kingdoms
along the hills and valleys of her hide.

❖ Contributors' Notes

Stacey Balkun is the author of *Jackalope-Girl Learns to Speak* (dancing girl 2016) & *Lost City Museum* (ELJ 2016). A Finalist for the 2016 Event Horizon Science Poetry Competition as well as the Center for Women Writer's 2016 Rita Dove Award, her work has appeared in *Crab Orchard Review, Gargoyle, Muzzle, Bayou*, and others. A 2015 Hambidge Fellow, Stacey served as Artist-in-Residence at the Great Smoky Mountains National Park in 2013. She holds an MFA from Fresno State and teaches poetry online at The Poetry Barn.

Devon Balwit is a poet and educator from Portland, Oregon. She has a chapbook, *Forms Most Marvelous*, (dancing girl press, 2017). Her recent poems can be found in: *Oyez, The Cincinnati Review, Red Paint Hill, The Ekphrastic Review, Noble Gas Quarterly, Timberline Review, Trailhead Magazine, Vector*, and *Permafrost*.

Annah Browning hails from the foothills of South Carolina. She holds a Ph.D. in English from the University of Illinois-Chicago, and is the author of a chapbook, *The Marriage* (Horse Less Press 2013). Her poems have appeared in *Indiana Review, Midwestern Gothic, Willow Springs*, and other journals, and have received awards and recognition from *Boulevard, Blue Mesa Review*, and *Vermont Studio Center*. She is an editor of *Grimoire*, an online literary magazine of dark arts.

Holly Burdorff is a VIDA volunteer and an MFA candidate in creative writing at the University of Alabama. Her work appears in recent or forthcoming issues of *Quarterly West, The Common, POOL, inter|rupture*, and *Cimarron Review*.

Steve Castro's poetry is forthcoming in *Plume*; *SurVision* (Ireland); *Forklift, Ohio* and was recently published in *[PANK] Magazine Online*; *Green Mountains Review, The American Journal of Poetry* and *Verse Daily*. He was recently interviewed by the *Chicago Review of Books*. Twitter: @PoetryEngineer

Author and illustrator, **Alan M. Clark** grew up in Tennessee in a house full of bones and old medical books. He has created illustrations for hundreds of books, including works of fiction of various genres, nonfiction, textbooks, young adult fiction, and children's books. Awards for his work include the World Fantasy Award and four Chesley Awards. He is the author of sixteen books, including eleven novels, a lavishly illustrated novella, four collections of fiction, and a nonfiction full-color book of his artwork. His latest novel, *Apologies to the Cat's Meat Man*, will was released in April of this year. Mr. Clark's company, IFD Publishing, has released 44 titles of various editions, including traditional books, audio books, and ebooks by such authors as F. Paul Wilson, Elizabeth Engstrom, and Jeremy Robert Johnson. Alan M. Clark and his wife, Melody, live in Oregon. www.alanmclark.com

Darren Demaree's poems have appeared, or are scheduled to appear in numerous magazines/journals, including the *South Dakota Review, Meridian, New Letters, Diagram*, and the *Colorado Review*. He is the author of six poetry collections, most recently *Many Full Hands Applauding Inelegantly* (8th House Publishing, 2016). He is the Managing Editor of the Best of the Net Anthology and Ovenbird Poetry. He lives in Columbus, Ohio with his wife and children.

Katie Dieter's writing has appeared in *The Atticus Review, Juked, Pleiades,* and *Prairie Schooner*, among other journals.

Andrew Dobbs is a tech entrepreneur and lives with his family in the small town of Wrentham, MA. This is his first major publication.

Jonathan Louis Duckworth received his MFA from Florida International University. His fiction, poetry, and non-fiction appears in *New Ohio Review, Fourteen Hills, PANK Magazine, Thrice Fiction, Cha, Superstition Review*, and elsewhere.

Samantha Edmonds is an MFA candidate at the University of Tennessee. Her work has previously appeared or is forthcoming in *Day One, Pleiades, The Indiana Review, Monkeybicycle*, and *McSweeney's Internet Tendency*, among others. Follow her on twitter: @sam_edmondsl22.

Delia Garigan was raised on a sheep farm and has spent time as a neuroscientist, Zen monastic, and teacher.

Giles Goodland was born in Taunton, was educated at the universities of Wales and California, took a D. Phil at Oxford, has published several books of poetry including *A Spy in the House of Years* (Leviathan, 2001) *Capital* (Salt, 2006) and *Dumb Messengers* (Salt, 2012). He works in Oxford as a lexicographer and lives in West London. His next book *The Masses* will be out from Shearsman in October 2017.

James Grabill's recent work is online at the *Caliban, Green Mountains Review, Kentucky Review, Elohi Gadugi, Buddhist Poetry Review, Harvard Review, Terrain, Mobius, Calliope, The Oxonian Review, The Toronto Quarterly, Mad Hatter's Review, Plumwood Mountain*, and others. His books include *Poem Rising Out of the Earth* (1994) and *An Indigo Scent after the Rain* (2003), both from Lynx House Press. Wordcraft of Oregon has published his new project of environmental prose poems, *Sea-Level Nerve: Book One*, 2014 and *Book Two*, 2015. A long-time Oregon resident, he teaches 'systems thinking' and global issues relative to sustainability.

Robert Guffey is a lecturer at California State University–Long Beach. His latest book is *Chameleo: A Strange but True Story of Invisible Spies, Heroin Addiction, and Homeland Security* (OR Books, 2015). A graduate of the Clarion Writers Workshop in Seattle, he has also written a collection of novellas entitled *Spies & Saucers* (PS Publishing, 2014). His first book of nonfiction, *Cryptoscatology: Conspiracy Theory as Art Form*, was published in 2012. He's written stories and articles for *The Believer, Catastrophia, The Chiron Review, The Los Angeles Review of Books, The Mailer Review, Pearl, The Pedestal, Phantom Drift, Postscripts*, and *The Third Alternative*. His first novel, *Until the Last Dogs*, is to be published by Night Shade/Skyhorse (November 2017).

Sarah Kain Gutowski is the author of *Fabulous Beast: The Sow*, a chapbook published by Hyacinth Girl Press, and a Professor of English at Suffolk County Community College. Her poems have been published in *Verse Daily, The Gettysburg Review, The Southern Review, Epiphany, The Threepenny Review*, and *So to Speak: A Feminist Journal of Language and Art*, and she has a review in the 40th anniversary issue of *Calyx: A Journal of Art and Literature by Women*. She keeps a record of her writing life, experience in academia, and motherhood at http://mimsyandoutgrabe.blogspot.com.

Seth Jani currently resides in Seattle, WA and is the founder of Seven Circle Press (www.sevencirclepress. com). His own work has been published widely in such places as *Abyss & Apex, The Devilfish Review, The Mithila Review, The Chiron Review, VAYAVYA, Gingerbread House* and *Gravel*. More about him and his work can be found at www.sethjani.com.

Chris Kammerud's work has appeared in *Dark Heart Volume 2: An Anthology of YA Dark Fairy Tales*, the *Interfictions Online Annex*, and multiple times in *Strange Horizons*. He is a graduate of the Clarion Writers' Workshop and received his MFA from the University of Mississippi. Along with his partner, he co-hosts a podcast about short stories called *Storyological*. He lives in London and, for the most part, avoids putting milk or honey in his tea.

Tricia Knoll is an Oregon poet with a long past of reading science fiction and fantasy. Occasionally she write pieces like these. She has two collections of poetry in print—*Ocean's Laughter* (Aldrich Press, 2016) and *Urban Wild* (Finishing Line Press, 2014). Website: triciaknoll.com

D. Lewis is an MFA candidate in Creative Writing at the University of Alabama.

Rebecca Lilly has poems in fairly recent issues of *Conjunctions*, and forthcoming in *Web Conjunctions* and *Denver Quarterly*. Within the past few years, she's taken up photography and is selling note cards and wall art at RebeccaLilly.com which features her photographic portfolios.

Kurt Luchs has poems published or forthcoming in *Into the Void, Fjords Review, Triggerfish Critical Review, Roanoke Review, Antiphon*, and *Emrys Journal*, among others. He won the 2017 Bermuda Triangle Poetry Prize. He founded the literary humor site TheBigJewel.com, and has written humor for the *New Yorker, the Onion* and *McSweeney's Internet Tendency*, as well as writing comedy for television (Politically Incorrect and the Late Late Show) and radio (American Comedy Network). Sagging Meniscus Press recently published his humor collection, *It's Funny Until Someone Loses an Eye (Then It's Really Funny)*.

Fiona Marshall is a writer and editor based in London. Her work has been published in a variety of outlets including *Prospect Magazine* and *The Royal Society of Literature Review*. She is the author of a novel, *Absence*.

Lindsey Martin-Bowen's third collection, *Crossing Kansas with Jim Morrison* (in chapbook form) was a semi-finalist in the QuillsEdge Press 2015-2016 Chapbook Contest. In late 2016, Writer's Digest gave her poem, "Vegetable Linguistics" an Honorable Mention. "Bonsai Tree Gone Awry" from her collection, *Inside Virgil's Garage* (Chatter House Press 2013) was nominated for a Pushcart Prize. McClatchy Newspapers named *Standing on the Edge of the World* (Woodley Press) one of the Ten Top Poetry Books of 2008. Paladin Contemporaries released three of her novels, the latest, *Rapture Redux*. She taught at University of Missouri-Kansas City 18 years and teaches at MCC-Longview. She holds MA and Juris Doctor degrees.

John A. McDermott's work has appeared in *Alaska Quarterly Review, The Pinch, Southeast Review*, and elsewhere. A native of Madison, Wisconsin, he now coordinates the BFA program in creative writing at Stephen F. Austin State University in Nacogdoches, Texas.

Nils Michals is the author of two collections of poetry, *Come Down to Earth* (Bauhan, 2014) and *Lure* (Pleiades, 2004). Individual poems have recently been published or are forthcoming in *PANK, Monday Night Lit, Posit, Four Chambers*, and *Small Po[r]tions*, among others. He lives in Santa Cruz and teaches at West Valley College. More information can be found at nilsmichals.com

GennaRose Nethercott is a poet, performer, and folklorist from the woodlands of Vermont. Her recent work has appeared in *The Offing, Rust & Moth, Cleaver*, and *Hermeneutic Chaos*, among others. She was named the grand prize winner of Spark Creative Anthology's poetry competition and the Lindenwood Review's flash fiction contest. She writes poems-to-order for passersby on a 1952 Hermes Rocket typewriter, a collection of which was released by Honeybee Press in 2015. GennaRose can be found at www.gennarosenethercott.com

Lynn Pattison's work has appeared in *The Notre Dame Review, Rhino, Harpur Palate, Smartish Pace, Slipstream*, and *Tinder Box* among others, and has been included in several anthologies. She is the author of three collections: *tesla's daughter* (March St. Press); *Walking Back the Cat* (Bright Hill Press) and *Light That Sounds Like Breaking* (Mayapple Press).

Tobias Peterson holds an MFA in Poetry from Texas State University. His work has appeared in *Analecta, The Indianola Review, The Gulf Coast Review, Coldnoon, Popmatters*, and elsewhere. He teaches at Clark College in Vancouver, Washington.

Nate Pritts is the Director and Founding Editor of H_NGM_N (2001), an independent publishing house that started as a mimeograph 'zine, and the author of eight books of poetry, including *Decoherence*, which won the 42 Miles Press Poetry Award and will be published in the fall of 2017. He lives in the Finger Lakes region of NY state.

Jennifer Pullen received her doctorate in Creative Writing from Ohio University in May 2017. She took a position as an Assistant Professor of Creative Writing at Ohio Northern University in August 2017. Her fiction and poetry have appeared or are upcoming in many journals, including a previous issue of *Phantom Drift*. Other anthologies and journals include, but are not limited to: *Clockhouse, Cleaver, Gravel, Prick of the Spindle*, and *Behind the Mask* (Meerkat Press).

C. Samuel Rees is a poet and educator living in Austin, Texas. His work has been featured by *The Fairy Tale Review, The Account, Borderlands: Texas Poetry Review, Raw Paw, Pithead Chapel, JMWW*, and *Peach Fuzz Magazine*. Recently his poem "Guten Abend, Gute Nacht" was nominated for a pushcart prize.

Lyle Roebuck is a novelist, essayist, and critic. Follow him on Twitter @LyleRoebuck.

J. J. Roth lives in the San Francisco Bay Area with her partner, two school-aged sons, and two geriatric cats. She parents the kids and cats, lawyers at a tech company, and writes literary speculative fiction in the interstices. J. J. is an associate member of the SFWA and a member of the Codex Writers Group. Her fiction has appeared in *Podcastle, Nature, Urban Fantasy Magazine*, and various semi-pro and small press venues. For more information and updates, please visit her web site at www.jjroth.net, follower her on Twitter where she is @wrothroth, or find her on Facebook, where she is JJ Roth.

David Russomano was awarded the Faber and Faber Creative Writing MA Prize in 2014 by Kingston University. In addition to being nominated for both The Pushcart Prize and Sundress Publications' 2012 Best of the Net Anthology, his poetry has appeared in various print and online publications, including *Poetry Quarterly, Structo,* and *Elbow Room.*

Miranda Schmidt's work has appeared or is forthcoming in *TriQuarterly, The Collagist, Phoebe, Luna Station Quarterly,* and other journals. Miranda lives with her wife and two cats in Portland, Oregon where she edits the *Sun Star Review* and teaches at Portland Community College. She is a graduate of the University of Washington's MFA program and a 2017 Lambda Literary Emerging LGBTQ Voices Fellow. Her recently completed novel was a finalist for the Nilsen First Novel Prize and she is currently at work on a project inspired by shapeshifting fairy tales. You can read more of her work at mirandaschmidt.com.

Matt Schumacher's latest book of poetry, *Ghost Town Odes,* was published last year by redbat books, and a chapbook, *favorite maritime drinking songs of the miraculous alcoholics,* appeared in print in 2015. His poetry has recently appeared in or is forthcoming in *Angel City Review, Ghost City Review,* and *The Offbeat.* He lives near a Paul Bunyan statue in Portland, Oregon.

Rose Servis lives in the Bay Area. She has fiction published in *Entropy, Phantom Drift,* and *Trop.*

John W. Sexton was born in 1958 and lives in the Republic of Ireland. His fifth poetry collection, *The Offspring of the Moon,* was published by Salmon Poetry in 2013. His sixth collection, *Futures Pass,* is also forthcoming from the same publisher. His poem "The Green Owl" was awarded the Listowel Poetry Prize 2007 for best single poem, and in that same year he was awarded a Patrick and Katherine Kavanagh Fellowship in Poetry. His poems are widely published and some have appeared in *Apex, The Edinburgh Review, The Irish Times, The Pedestal Magazine, Phantom Drift, Poetry Ireland Review, Rose Red Review* and *Strange Horizons.*

Virginia Shreve, who once penned an entire catalogue devoted solely to corrugated office products resides in the small river town of Collinsville, CT, with husband and dogs, none well-trained, but all good-natured. For years, she wrote and edited numerous regional newsletters, much dog humor, and her poems have appeared in *The Southern Poetry Review,* the *Naugatuck River Review, Slippery Elm,* and others. Her poem "Tintype" was nominated for a Pushcart Prize.

Armin Tolentino received his MFA at Rutgers University in Newark, NJ. His poetry has appeared, or is forthcoming, in *Arsenic Lobster, Common Knowledge,* and *The Raven Chronicles.* He's an Oregon Literary Arts Fellowship recipient and works in anti-poverty and education programming in Portland. When not writing, he spends way too much time fishing (call it "research") and rooting for the Knicks, both futile endeavors.

Tom Weller is a former factory worker, Peace Corps volunteer, Planned Parenthood sexuality educator, and college writing instructor who recently relocated to Lock Haven, Pennsylvania. His fiction and creative nonfiction have appeared in a variety of journals and anthologies including *Litro, Epiphany, Phantom Drift, Paper Darts, Silk Road, Booth,* and *One Hand Does Not Catch a Buffalo: Fifty Years of Amazing Peace Corps Stories.*

IT'S YOUR IMAGINATION

FEED IT

PHANTOM DRIFT

Accepting Submissions for Issue No. 8
January 1 – April 30, 2018

Please read guidelines carefully before submitting, then submit your
fabulist story, poem, or critical essay through our website at:
www.phantomdrift.org

Fiction:
$5 per page (minimum $10)

Poetry:
$5 per page (minimum $10)

Nonfiction:
$5 per page (minimum $10)

WE AT
PHANTOM DRIFT

GIVE A MONSTROUS

S H O U T O U T

TO CONTRIBUTORS,
DONORS AND
SUBSCRIBERS,
FOR BELIEVING IN US.
WE COULDN'T MANIFEST
WITHOUT YOU.

THANKS!!!

www.ingramcontent.com/pod-product-compliance
Lightning Source LLC
Chambersburg PA
CBHW080759250626
47159CB00011B/3448